THE GAME OF THE GOOSE

In her hand was a hinged wooden box with a black clasp.
On the lid was a painting of a white bird with a long
neck, its wings stretched out in flight. Fred rubbed it
with her fingers, wiping away the dust.
'The Game of the Goose,' she read slowly.
'Open it,' said Rowley . . .

Fred, Rowley and Rabbit hardly knew each other
before the game. But the game changed everything.
It took each of them on an adventure – a terrifying,
wonderful journey that they would remember for ever.

ALSO BY URSULA DUBOSARSKY

The Red Shoe
Theodora's Gift
Abyssinia
How to be a Great Detective
My Father is not a Comedian!
Black Sails, White Sails
Zizzy Zing
Bruno and the Crumhorn
The First Book of Samuel
The White Guinea Pig
The Last Week in December
High Hopes

PICTURE BOOKS:
Rex
Illustrated by David Mackintosh
Honey and Bear
Special Days with Honey and Bear
Illustrated by Ron Brooks

AUSSIE BITES
The Strange Adventures of Isador Brown
The Even Stranger Adventures of Isador Brown
Isador Brown's Strangest Adventures of All
Illustrated by Paty Marshall-Stace

AUSSIE NIBBLES
The Two Gorillas
Fairy Bread
The Puppet Show
The Magic Wand
Illustrated By Mitch Vane

THE
GAME
OF THE
GOOSE

URSULA
DUBOSARSKY

with illustrations by
John Winch

PUFFIN BOOKS

PUFFIN BOOKS

Published by the Penguin Group
Penguin Group (Australia)
250 Camberwell Road
Camberwell, Victoria 3124, Australia
(a division of Pearson Australia Group Pty Ltd)
Penguin Group (USA) Inc.
375 Hudson Street, New York, New York 10014, USA
Penguin Group (Canada)
90 Eglinton Avenue East, Suite 700,
Toronto ON M4P 2Y3, Canada
(a division of Pearson Penguin Canada Inc.)
Penguin Books Ltd
80 Strand, London WC2R 0RL, England
Penguin Ireland
25 St Stephen's Green, Dublin 2, Ireland
(a division of Penguin Books Ltd)
Penguin Books India Pvt Ltd
11, Community Centre, Panchsheel Park, New Delhi -110 017, India
Penguin Group (NZ)
67 Apollo Drive, Rosedale, North Shore 0632, New Zealand
(a division of Pearson New Zealand Ltd)
Penguin Books (South Africa) (Pty) Ltd
24 Sturdee Avenue, Rosebank, Johannesburg 2196, South Africa

Penguin Books Ltd, Registered Offices: 80 Strand, London WC2R 0RL, England

First published by Penguin Books Australia, 2000
This edition published by Penguin Group (Australia),
a division of Pearson Australia Group Pty Ltd, 2007

5 7 9 10 8 6 4

Cover design by Elizabeth Dias, Penguin Design Studio
Cover illustration by Tracie Grimwood
Typeset in 13/17pt Bembo by Midland Typesetters Maryborough, Victoria
Printed in Australia by McPherson's Printing Group, Maryborough, Victoria

National Library of Australia
Cataloguing-in-Publication data:

Dubosarsky, Ursula, 1961- .
The game of the goose.

ISBN 9780141309231 (pbk.).

1. Board games - Juvenile fiction. I. Title.

A823.3

puffin.com.au

For Sebastian, Madeleine and Phoebe,
with lots of love.

This edition dedicated to the memory of John Winch.

'Hope' is the thing with feathers
That perches in the soul
And sings the tune without the words
And never stops – at all

And sweetest in the Gale is heard
And sore must be the storm
That could abash the little Bird
That kept so many warm

I've heard it in the chillest land
And on the strangest Sea
Yet, never, in Extremity
It asked a crumb – of Me

EMILY DICKINSON

· 1 ·

Before

There were three children: Fred, Rowley and Rabbit. Fred was a girl, Rowley was a boy, and Rabbit was small. Rabbit was a boy, too, but because he was only six, sometimes the others forgot.

Fred, Rowley and Rabbit were all only children – they didn't have any brothers or sisters. They lived next door to one other in three different houses, but they didn't know each other, not really.

Fred and Rowley sometimes looked at each other through the cracks in the fence. Fred could see Rowley's mud-brick cubby-house that his father had built him, and she felt quite jealous. But when Rowley peered back, he saw Fred bouncing up and down on her trampoline and he felt jealous enough himself.

Rabbit could see both things at once, because he could climb up into the branches of a very tall tree on the edge of his own fence and look down on them, like a blackbird. Fred and Rabbit actually did know each other just a little bit – once, Rabbit had been left to stay the night at Fred's house, and he slept on the floor in Fred's room. Rabbit came with his pyjamas and his toothbrush which had a plastic shark on the end of it. He cleaned his teeth all the time, even in his sleep.

The fence that ran between the houses was very old. In some parts it was falling forwards or backwards, in some places it was quite sunk down and in some places there were holes where the wood had rotted away to nothing. The children didn't ever really think about it – it was just a fence – but the parents hated it. They thought it was ugly and dangerous.

So one summer holiday, when it was very hot and boring, Fred's parents went and saw Rowley's parents and Rowley's parents went and saw Rabbit's parents, and all the parents decided it was time to build a new fence. They made some telephone calls and in no time at all a truckload of people arrived with axes. They chopped down the fence and put the remains in the back of the truck and drove away.

The children looked outside and suddenly instead of three small gardens there was one enormous backyard with no fence at all, and they could all see right into each other's houses.

At first, each of them stayed in their own garden,

just as though the fence were still there but invisible, like a magic line they couldn't cross over.

Rowley kicked his soccer ball up and down by himself as he usually did. Fred bounced on her trampoline. She did lots of somersaults, because she knew Rowley was watching even if he was pretending not to.

Rabbit climbed up the tall grey tree with no leaves and called out in a strange high little voice:

'Hallo! Hallo! Hallo!'

Rowley kept kicking the ball and Fred kept bouncing. Because Rabbit was so small they didn't have to say hallo back.

But Rabbit kept on calling out in his funny little voice: 'Hallo! Hallo! Hallo!'

He didn't get any higher or lower or crosser. In fact, he sounded as though he could probably go on calling out 'Hallo!' all day long, so, to make him stop, Fred finally bounced off the trampoline, went over to the tree and said, 'Hallo!'

Then Rabbit didn't say anything, he just went all silent and stared at her.

Fred shrugged. She scratched her head. Perhaps Rabbit didn't even remember sleeping on the floor of her room with his toothbrush in his mouth.

Now she was very close to where Rowley was kicking his ball, but the invisible line was between them. Rowley didn't look up. He kicked the ball one way and then the other. He paused for a moment, the ball under his foot.

Then, without warning, almost by accident, he kicked it right over to where Fred stood. At once, automatically, she kicked it back.

Rabbit laughed and clapped his hands. Rowley kicked the ball again and Fred started to run and kicked it back. The magic line between the houses disappeared. Soon they were running all over the three backyards as though it were a soccer field and the trampoline was one goal and the wall outside Rowley's kitchen was the other.

After a while, panting and red-faced, they stopped. Fred threw herself onto the ground on her back. Rowley stood directly beneath the sun holding the ball under one arm.

Rabbit, who had been watching the whole time, climbed down from his tree, crossed the invisible fence and ran over to Rowley and Fred.

'This is the biggest backyard in the world!' cried Fred in delight, rolling down the sloping earth, covering her clothes with grass and dead leaves.

'It's as big as a millionaire's backyard!' said Rowley, kicking the ball as high as he could.

Rabbit looked up. The ball was so far away he thought it would reach the sun and melt. But then it started to come down again and he screamed and ran for cover under his tree.

Even their pets seemed to realise the magic line had disappeared. Fred's white cat went and ate food from the bowl of Rabbit's grey cat, and Rabbit's cat went and lay down on Rowley's back verandah.

Rowley didn't have a cat because he was allergic, but he had a dark-brown guinea-pig called Jemima Puddleduck. Usually she ran around by herself in Rowley's backyard but now that she had three times the space she scuttled all over the place and still didn't get tired.

'She's a Restless Cavy,' explained Rowley. 'It means guinea-pig-who-never-sleeps.'

'That's unnatural,' said Fred, frowning. 'You have to sleep.'

'Jemima doesn't,' said Rowley. 'And she's part of nature, so it must be natural.'

'She's lucky,' said Rabbit. 'She mustn't ever have nightmares.'

'Guinea-pigs don't dream,' said Fred, scornfully.

'Everything dreams,' said Rabbit, because he was sure they must.

'Well, not Jemima,' said Rowley, 'because she never sleeps.'

They lay on their backs and looked up at the sky. It was such a hot summer and there were no clouds. It was too hot even for daydreams.

· 2 ·

The Secret Word

Now, the parents had planned that the next day some more people would arrive in another truck full of new fence-posts and hammers. They would dig deep holes and hammer the posts into the ground, so all three houses would have beautiful new fences.

But far away in the middle of the night, something wonderful happened. Well, wonderful from the point of view of the children, that is; not their parents. The factory where all the fence-posts were made burnt down in a mysterious fire. This meant the new posts wouldn't be ready for another month.

All the parents came out into the enormous back-yard to talk about the disaster. On and on they went, shaking their heads, throwing their arms about. How could this happen! What bad luck! Wouldn't you know it!

Fred, Rowley and Rabbit ran over to each other, eyes shining.

'There won't be any new fence-posts for a month!' said Rowley.

'The whole holidays!' said Fred with a little leap.

'Maybe forever!' said Rabbit longingly, because he was so lonely in his own house.

The parents began to drift with hunched shoulders back inside, deep in disappointment.

Rowley said, 'Let's have a club.'

Rabbit took a few steps backward towards his tree.

'Oh yes!' agreed Fred.

Rabbit started to climb up the tree.

'We need a headquarters,' said Fred, and she looked meaningfully at Rowley's mud-brick cubby-house.

'Are you scared of spiders?' asked Rowley.

Fred shook her head. 'I like spiders,' she said.

Rabbit said from up the tree, 'I eat spiders!'

'Come on in, I'll show you,' said Rowley.

Fred followed Rowley over to the cubby-house. The doorway was low and jagged and they had to bend down. Inside, the roof was higher and they could just stand up. It was dark and hot and smelt of trees.

Rowley lit a candle that was stuck in the mouth of an empty bottle. Fred looked around for spiders. Then she heard some very strange deep breathing. It was only Rabbit, standing at the door of the cubby, looking in.

Rowley smiled. 'Come on in,' he said kindly, holding out his hand. 'Don't be scared.'

Rabbit did not have to bend like the others, he just walked straight in. 'I can't see any spiders,' he said, looking around. 'There's nothing here at all.'

He was right, there was nothing, apart from the candle in the bottle and a box of matches. There wasn't even anything to sit on.

'It's perfect!' said Fred.

'There's nothing to do,' said Rabbit, sitting down on the dirt floor.

'We can bring things,' said Rowley. 'We can each go home and bring things back here.'

So they did. Fred brought books, a pencil case, paper and a game of Monopoly with most of the pieces missing. She also brought half a packet of chocolate biscuits.

Rowley brought a kite and some more empty bottles and a pile of comics. The most important thing he brought was a short wooden stool which he put in the middle of the room.

'This can be a table,' he said.

Rabbit brought very strange things – a brand-new bar of yellow soap and a calendar from 1987. He smuggled them out of his house in his shorts, in case he wasn't allowed.

Rowley put the bottle with the candle in it on the

stool. It rocked about a bit and the flame flickered on their hot faces. They felt like they were burning up.

Fred got out a pencil and started writing on a piece of paper.

'What are you doing?' asked Rabbit.

'I'm writing about the club,' said Fred. 'What are we going to call ourselves?'

They sat and thought. Nobody wanted to say anything, in case their idea wasn't good.

'I think it should be a secret name,' said Fred after a while.

'What do you mean?' asked Rowley.

'A secret name that we all know,' explained Fred, 'but that is never spoken out loud.'

'How do we know it then?' asked Rabbit.

'I'll whisper it in your ear,' said Fred. 'And then you whisper it in Rowley's ear, and then we'll all know.'

Rabbit looked excited. He jumped up and leaned towards Fred, putting his hot little ear right up against her lips. Fred whispered. Rabbit frowned. Fred whispered again.

'I can't hear!' complained Rabbit.

Fred whispered for the third time, a cross whisper. 'And if you didn't hear that you can't be in the club!' she snapped loudly.

Rabbit bit his lip. His eyes grew round and he

blinked several times. Then he took a deep breath and leaned over to Rowley and whispered in his ear.

'What?' said Rowley.

Rabbit nodded.

'That's it!' he said.

Rowley rolled his eyes and shrugged and said, 'All right. If you say so.'

They were quiet for a little while. The only sounds were the cicadas in the trees outside, and Fred's scribbling pencil.

'There!' she said at last. She held up the piece of paper in the candlelight. This is what she had written:

CLUB RULES

1. The name of the club is a secret.
2. Everything in the clubhouse has to be shared, except for special things.
3. Only people over the age of seven can light the candle.
4. Do NOT kill any spiders, because it is very bad luck.

'What counts as 'special things'?' asked Rowley, reading over her shoulder.

'Whatever the person who owns it says,' replied Fred. She knew what her special things were, including the chocolate biscuits.

Rabbit was staring at the list with large frightened eyes.

'Sorry about rule number three, Rabbit,' said Fred. 'It's for safety.'

Rabbit looked hard at the number three. 'I can't read,' he said, shaking his head.

'You can't read!' Fred was scandalised.

'I'm only six,' whimpered Rabbit.

'I could read when I was six,' said Fred. 'I could read when I was four!'

'I try,' said poor Rabbit. 'But I just can't!'

Rowley reached over and screwed the piece of paper into a ball. 'I hate rules,' he said, tossing it on the floor.

'What did you do that for?!' said Fred angrily.

'It's my cubby,' retorted Rowley, 'and I say, NO RULES.'

Fred kicked the floor with her toes. 'Well, that's a rule for a start,' she muttered darkly at the muddy walls.

It was as bad as having brothers and sisters. And because none of them had ever had brothers and sisters, they were each used to getting their own way.

Fred felt angry with Rowley – so angry she wanted to kill him. Still, she decided after a while, it's better to fight a bit than be bored to death. For Fred, boredom was the worst thing in the world.

For Rowley the worst thing in the world was school.

And for Rabbit? Rabbit wasn't sure what the worst thing was, he was still thinking about it.

· 3 ·

The Moneybox

The next day was even hotter than before. The three of them sat inside the cubby. It was too hot to move. Jemima Puddleduck lay like a puddle in a dark heap in the corner. Rowley picked up Fred's battered Monopoly set.

'We need some good games,' he said. 'I hate Monopoly.'

Fred was sweating. She stood up and looked out into the huge garden. 'Let's dig a hole,' she said, 'and fill it with water for a swimming pool.'

Now that was a wonderful idea! They could build their own club swimming pool! Rowley ran down to his back shed and fetched a couple of shovels, while Rabbit brought a plastic bucket and spade from his sandpit.

They looked around for a good spot to put the pool.

'In the middle,' said Fred, 'so when the fences go back up we can all use it.'

Rowley felt somehow this didn't quite make sense – the fence had to go somewhere, so wouldn't the pool end out in someone's backyard?

'All right,' he said. He stuck the spade into the earth. It was as hard as concrete. 'It's so dry! It's impossible to dig like this.'

He looked up at the sun, shading his eyes. It hadn't rained for days, and didn't look like it would ever again.

Fred said, 'I'll bring the hose.'

Rabbit stood with his bucket and spade, watching, fascinated. He would never dare turn the hose on all by himself! Fred tugged it over like the lead of a reluctant dog. She was fiddling with the nozzle.

'How do you get the water to come out?' she said, half to herself.

Then, of course, the water did come out, all over her, but she didn't care because she was so hot it was a relief. Just to be friendly she sprayed water all over Rowley as well and he got as wet as wet, and then she put tiny sprays on Rabbit because she didn't want to get into trouble with his mother.

'Oh children, children!' cried Fred's mother, looking out from the kitchen window where she was chopping onions.

She came tearing down to where they were digging, still with the knife in her hand. Poor little Rabbit thought she might be going to stab them because he didn't know Fred's mother very well, only from that time he stayed the night and that was awful because she made him eat mashed potato. So he screamed and ran straight over to hide behind his tree.

'It was an accident!' Fred wailed.

Fred's mother stood there with her knife gleaming and she put up one hand to wipe the sweat and onion tears from her face and she said, 'It's so *hot*! You poor children. I suppose it'll cool you down.'

'I could spray you too, if you like,' suggested Fred helpfully.

'No thanks,' replied Fred's mother. 'But there's something you could do for me – you could run up to the shops and get some more milk.'

They were always running out of milk. Fred loved milk. She drank enough to feed a calf.

'All right,' said Fred and she turned to Rowley. 'Do you want to come?'

Rowley shrugged and said he might as well.

'Can I come too?' came Rabbit's voice from behind the tree. Fred's mother looked over with a smile.

'Oh! Rabbit! I wondered where you'd got to!'

'Can I come?' repeated Rabbit, coming slowly out into the open.

'You'd better ask your mother,' said Fred's mother.

'She's asleep,' replied Rabbit.

'Oh dear.' Fred's mother frowned and sighed and waved the knife about.

'Please let me go!' begged Rabbit. 'Mummy won't mind!'

Fred looked at Rowley as if to say, Mummy mightn't mind, but what about us?

'I've got some money,' said Rabbit, catching their glance. 'I've got my life-savings in my moneybox.'

'Oh, let him come,' Fred said to her mother. 'We'll look after him.'

'You've got to hold his hand crossing the road,' said Fred's mother, giving in.

So Rabbit came.

· 4 ·

Finding the Game

They met on the footpath in front of their houses. Fred had a string bag and a shopping list. Rowley brought his wallet in case he saw something he wanted. Rabbit was wearing a big black and white spotty sunhat so you could hardly see his face, and he was clutching a moneybox in the shape of an elephant. He looked terribly excited.

The shops were not far, but they had to cross two streets and a set of traffic lights. Fred held Rabbit's hand, which was fierce and sweaty. They went into the supermarket and bought milk and bread and bananas and Rowley bought a bag of carrots for Jemima.

'Maybe we could get an ice-cream,' said Fred. 'We could go and sit in the park.'

They all liked the sound of that. But as they turned the corner, they came to a stop outside the Salvation

Army second-hand shop. It had a big window full of things – bits of dusty furniture, cups and saucers, coats and shoes.

'Let's go in here first,' said Rowley. 'There might be some good toys. For the clubhouse, you know.'

'All right,' said Fred.

They went inside. The shop was crowded; not with people, but shelves and boxes and trolleyfuls of things. There was a television on in one corner and a great collection of umbrellas in the other, and there was a musty smell.

Fred, Rowley and Rabbit squeezed through to the toys, which were piled on top of each other in big open suitcases, just under the payment counter. They put down their shopping bags, knelt and began sifting through the bits and pieces.

'What a lot of rubbish,' said Rowley, sniffing. 'Everything looks about a hundred years old!'

'Here's a ping-pong net!' said Fred, lifting it up from inside a case. 'Maybe there're bats as well. We could set it up in the cubby and have a tournament.'

'We don't have a table,' said Rowley, but he reached down under and started looking.

'So many of these horrible squeaky toys,' muttered Fred. 'I don't believe anyone likes those toys. Have you ever seen a baby squeak one?'

'Look!' said Rabbit, in a soft, whispering voice from under his spotty hat.

Rabbit was on the other side of the suitcase. He had a drawstring bag in his hand and was feeling the lumps.

'What is it?' asked Rowley, crawling over to him.

'It's animals,' said Rabbit. 'Lots of them.'

He emptied the bag onto the floor and out tumbled a gang of little felt animals in different colours and shapes, stuffed with rice. Rowley looked over his shoulder.

'It's a Noah's Ark,' he said. 'See – there's Noah and there's the little boat.'

'Noah's Ark!' Rabbit repeated the words.

He sat back on his heels and began to line the pieces up on the floor. Rowley left him to it and went back to join Fred in her search for ping-pong bats.

But Fred had stopped looking – she had found something else.

'Rowley,' she said, tugging at his sleeve.

In her hand was a hinged wooden box with a black clasp. On the lid was a painting of a white bird with a long neck, its wings stretched out in flight. Fred rubbed it with her fingers, wiping away the dust. Underneath the bird were written some words in gold.

'The Game of the Goose,' read Fred slowly.

'Open it,' said Rowley.

Fred's fingers reached down to the clasp to tug it open. It was rusted and stiff. Suddenly, she stopped.

'What's that?' she said, holding her fingers still.

'What?' said Rowley.

'Can't you hear that?'

'No,' said Rowley.

Fred shivered. She got up from the floor, the box under her arm.

'I'm going to buy it,' she said.

Rowley got up as well. Rabbit was still down there somewhere, singing a little song to the line of felt animals. Fred put the Game down on the counter. A man was sitting reading the newspaper behind an old-fashioned cash register.

'How much is this?' asked Fred.

The man pointed at a little yellow sticker on the side of the box.

'That's the price,' he said.

Fred bit her lip. She knew how much change she had left from her mother's shopping. It would not be enough.

'That's too much!' she cried.

'That's the price,' replied the man, uninterested.

'But it's old!' complained Rowley.

'Well, yes, it is old,' said the man, rolling his eyes. 'That's the point. It's an antique. Can't give it away.'

Fred turned to Rowley. 'How much have you got?'

Rowley took out his wallet and emptied the coins onto the counter. Fred did the same. The man raised his eyebrows.

'Not enough,' he said, and went back to his newspaper.

'But I have to have it!' wailed Fred. 'Let us have it! No one else wants it!'

The man shook his head firmly, not looking up. 'That's the price.'

Fred was desperate. She had to have the Game, although she couldn't explain why. All the space in her head was taken up with the need for it. She looked down at Rabbit. She picked up the Game from the counter and knelt beside him.

'Rabbit!'

Rabbit was humming.

'Rabbit!' Fred said urgently. 'Look at this!'

Rabbit was hard to reach; he was in the middle of a game of his own.

'Rabbit!' Fred shook his shoulders.

Rabbit looked up at her dreamily. 'What?'

'Look at this,' said Fred. 'It's a game.' She held up the box to show him.

'What sort of a game?' asked Rabbit, not really looking. He wanted to play with the animals. He was making up a story.

'It's this wonderful game, Rabbit,' said Fred, cajoling. 'We can all play it together. It'll be great.'

'Hmmmm,' said Rabbit.

'It's a board game – you know, you throw the dice and move the pieces.'

Fred had not even seen inside the box, but somehow she felt she knew all about it.

'But much better than Monopoly,' put in Rowley, coming over and kneeling next to her.

'Rabbit – let's buy it!' said Fred. 'Come on, Rowley and I've put in all our money – you put in the rest. Go on!'

Rabbit's hands went instinctively to his elephant moneybox.

'I want to buy the Noah's Ark,' he said in a small voice.

'Oh, Rabbit – this is much better. We can all play this!' Fred sounded very high.

'It's not even complete,' said Rowley, meaning the Noah's Ark. 'There's not two of every animal. See?' He pointed to where Rabbit had laid them out. 'There's only one bird, and look, this one's leaking . . .' As Rowley shook it, grains of rice scattered over the floor.

'That's the dove,' said Rabbit, snatching it back. 'There's only meant to be one.'

'Oh, Rabbit!' Rowley groaned. 'It's yellow. There's no such thing as a yellow dove.'

'It's home-made!' said Fred scornfully.

'There's not even a Mrs Noah,' added Rowley.

Rabbit was silent. His hand tightened around his moneybox. Fred and Rowley exchanged glances.

'Please, Rabbit,' said Fred.

Rabbit pointed at the Game with one of his tiny fingers. 'What does that say?' he asked.

'The Game of the Goose,' said Fred. 'See the picture of the goose?'

'Not that bit,' said Rabbit, shaking his head. '*That* bit.'

He traced his fingertip along some dark lettering on the edge of the box.

Fred squinted. She had not seen the words under the dust – the letters were so faded. She read out loud: 'The Race is Not Always to the Swift, Nor the Battle to the Strong.'

Rabbit listened carefully and then he said, 'What does that mean?'

'It's just words!' said Fred impatiently.

'It means that it's not always the fastest or the strongest person who wins,' explained Rowley.

'Oh.' Rabbit nodded and thought about it. 'Like the Hare and the Tortoise.'

Then none of them said anything for a moment. They were waiting for Rabbit. But Rabbit had a hard expression in his eyes.

'We'll let you have first turn,' pleaded Fred at last.

'Go on, Rabbit,' said Rowley. He leant down and began to tug at the moneybox. The hard little expression on Rabbit's face suddenly changed and became frightened.

'But I want the Noah's Ark,' he said, his voice even smaller. 'I want it. There won't be enough money for both.'

'We should get something we all like,' said Fred, 'not just what you like.' She reached down and eased the moneybox out of Rabbit's fingers. He let go, his hands fell to his sides. Fred stood up and put it with the Game on the counter. She opened the bottom of the moneybox and tipped out all the coins, and she and Rowley counted them up.

The man selling looked up from his newspaper and said, 'Well, well, well.' He swept all the money into his hand. He took off the yellow sticker from the Game and put it into a plastic bag. Rabbit watched without a word.

'Enjoy yourselves,' said the man.

Fred grabbed the bag, then picked up her other bag of milk and bread and bananas from the floor.

'Come on,' she said roughly to Rowley. She did not look at Rabbit. Rowley gave Rabbit a little slap on the shoulder and said, 'Come on. Let's go back to the clubhouse.'

They left the shop and walked all the way home, nobody saying anything. Fred made sure she held Rabbit's hand when they crossed the road, both times, but it felt cold and empty of life, like a glove.

· 5 ·

Skeletons

When they got back, they each walked quickly in their own front door, slamming it behind them, like three little mechanical cuckoos in three different clocks.

Fred took the shopping into the kitchen and put the milk in the fridge. She went into the bathroom and splashed water all over her face – she could not remember feeling so hot, not even when she was ill.

Then she ran out to the clubhouse, the Game of the Goose under her arm.

Rowley was already there. He had lit the candle, but it was still dark as a church. He had brought some old cushions and was sitting on one next to the stool.

Fred sat down opposite him, and laid the Game of the Goose carefully on the stool.

Her throat tightened. It was like getting a letter in

the mail that you had been waiting for forever.

'Well, are you going to open it?' said Rowley.

Fred reached over, her hand trembling, and undid the clasp. She could not understand how she was feeling. Her mind felt bright yellow and floating somewhere above her.

The box swung open. And it happened again! That sound she had heard back in the shop. There was a ringing in her ears, like a distant high whistling.

'There!' she turned quickly to Rowley, her voice hoarse. 'Did you hear it this time?'

Rowley grimaced. He did hear – something. But it was very faint. Already it had stopped.

They stared down at the box. Inside were three pieces of flat wood. Fred took them out and put them together in a row, so that all the right parts joined with each other like a jigsaw.

'It's the playing board,' she said.

How it glowed! It looked like an old map. Up the top in the middle was written THE GAME OF THE GOOSE, with the picture of the flying goose next to it. Underneath the goose was a beautiful tiny picture of a castle, with turrets and domes and flags waving in a wind.

'Look!' said Rowley, raising the candle and bringing it close. He screwed up his eyes to see.

Underneath the castle was a red star and the words

START HERE. Then, coming out from the star were three paths which wound in different directions all over the board. Each path was made up of numbered paving stones. They curled and twisted and overlapped and, at various points, like in Snakes and Ladders, there were messages and figures and special directions written in spiky black writing.

Fred put her fingertips over the board, feeling it as though it were a book written in braille. The background was painted golden and green, and along the paths were drawn some wonderful things – The Magic Sea, The Island of Children, The Peacock Forest . . . But there were also frightening things – The Maze of Despair, The Cold Tower, The Ice Storm . . .

Rowley leant down and read aloud from the board. 'The Old City . . . miss a turn and proceed to number 17 . . . Go around Spiral . . . The Whispering Market . . . land at number 75 . . . wait till a 3 or 5 is thrown . . . Is there a dice, Fred?'

Fred was dazed, her eyes wide and unblinking.

'A dice?' she said. 'I don't know – maybe in here.'

Inside the box was another box. It was also wooden but much smaller and with a lid that slid open. Inside it was a golden die with silver dots for numbers.

'It's so heavy!' said Rowley, taking the cube and weighing it up in his hand. 'Like it's really gold.'

Fred said, 'These must be the pieces.'

She tipped the smaller box upside-down onto the table and out tumbled three glittering trinkets, tinkling as they fell. The first was a little key. The second was a tiny dagger with a braided belt. The third was a minute pair of silver shoes with wings on the heels, held together by a piece of string.

Fred and Rowley looked at each other in wonder.

'That's why it cost so much,' said Rowley. 'They're like jewels.'

'Each player must have to choose one,' said Fred, glancing back at the board. 'See, it's written here – The Key. The Girdle. The Shoes of Swiftness.'

'What's a girdle?' said Rowley.

'It's a kind of belt,' replied Fred. 'And the knife hangs off it. See?'

'And then you choose a path,' said Rowley. 'Each person goes on a different path.'

'How do you win?' wondered Fred. 'What happens at the end?'

Rowley bent his head right over the darkness of the board, till his nose was almost touching it.

'I think . . . Here, look, the paths all finish up together at the bottom. There's some sort of bridge . . . It's so hard to see . . .'

Suddenly, he stopped talking and sat up again. He looked frightened.

'What is it?' said Fred.

'It looks like . . . I don't know,' Rowley said, and his face closed over in secrets.

'Like what?'

'I don't know,' said Rowley again. Then he said, 'Like skeletons or something. Like a skull.'

'Skeletons?' Fred grimaced at the board. It was so dirty, she couldn't see anything. Why would there be skeletons? She stared at the place where all the paths met at the bottom of the board for a long time.

'I don't see anything,' she said at last, and she raised her eyes to Rowley, her expression blank. 'I don't know what you're talking about.'

'Fred,' began Rowley, hesitating. 'Maybe we shouldn't –'

'Shouldn't what?' said Fred at once.

But Rowley wasn't sure what he meant. He was afraid, that was all.

'Are you too scared to play?' said Fred.

The flame of the candle flickered. Rowley bit his lip.

'No,' he said. 'Let's play.'

· 6 ·

The Game Begins

'You said I could go first,' came a voice from the darkness.

Fred started, knocking the candle over. Hot wax oozed onto her fingers.

It was Rabbit. He was standing just inside the door, his big brown eyes glistening in the dark.

'How long have you been there?' Fred said with a scowl, righting the candle.

Rabbit shuffled over to the table. He looked at them and then down at the board and then at them again.

'You said I could go first,' he repeated.

'Of course you can,' said Rowley, easily. 'We were waiting for you.'

'No you weren't,' said Rabbit.

Nobody said anything.

'You were going to play without me,' said Rabbit.

'We were not!' retorted Fred, finding her voice. 'We didn't know where you were. You just ran off.'

Rabbit sat down in front of the board and crossed his legs. He looked at the little shining pieces.

'What are they?' he asked, pointing, not quite daring to touch.

'They're like the counters,' said Rowley.

'You're a bully,' said Rabbit to Fred. 'My mother says. And so are you,' he added to Rowley.

'So you told your mother?' Fred was outraged.

'My mother's asleep,' replied Rabbit, huffily. Then he added, 'But she knows.'

'Come on, Rabbit, forget it. Why don't you choose a piece and we can play.' Rowley was relieved and gave him a little push. To his own surprise he was glad that Rabbit was there to play as well.

'You took all my money,' muttered Rabbit, but he was distracted by the beauty of the Game, and the glittering charms. He forgot for a moment what he was angry about. 'What are the rules?'

'There aren't any rules,' said Fred. 'You pick a piece. Then you pick a path. Then you throw the dice.'

'That's rules,' said Rabbit.

Fred shrugged.

'Then what?' said Rabbit.

'Then – then you just – follow it . . .' Fred supposed

that's what you did. It had to be, there was nothing else to do. 'You just see what happens,' she said, and she paused. 'Right to the end.'

She looked Rowley in the eye, as if she were challenging him to say something.

'Can I be the winner?' said Rabbit.

'It's just luck, Rabbit,' said Rowley. 'You can't make somebody win. It depends what you land on.'

Rabbit was unconvinced. 'I want to be the winner,' he said.

'All right, fine! Be the winner! Who cares!' Fred thought she would go mad. 'Can we just play!'

'Go on, Rabbit,' said Rowley. 'Just play. You can go first. Go on.'

Rabbit sniffed. He rubbed his eyes with his fists. Then he touched each of the charms in turn. He took for ever. Fred thought she might hit him.

'I pick –'

He stopped.

'I pick –'

He stopped again.

'Get on with it, will you!' Fred screamed, because she had to have the girdle, she just had to, she would die if Rabbit took it.

'I pick the key!' said Rabbit at last. 'And I pick Path Number One.' He put the key down carefully on the first step of that path.

'And I pick the girdle,' cried Fred, seizing it.

'It looks like I'm having the shoes of swiftness,' said Rowley happily, not caring what he had. But which path? His hand hovered above the board.

'You take Number Two,' said Fred quickly. 'I'll be lucky last.'

They each put their pieces down on the board. They were ready.

'Well, then,' said Fred. 'Go on, Rabbit. Throw the dice. Let's play.'

Rabbit picked up the die. He squeezed it and gave his fist a kiss as he had seen his father do playing backgammon. Then he held it over the board and let it drop.

The die fell. It rolled and rolled until finally it came to a stop.

'Six!' shouted Rabbit in delight, who, although he could not read, could count at least.

Then he picked up the magic key and began to move along the squares.

'One, two, three, four, five –'

And as he said the word 'six' and laid the key on that number on the board, Rabbit disappeared from sight.

So began the Game of the Goose.

· 7 ·

The Magic Sea

Rabbit disappeared from the sight of Fred and Rowley, but he didn't disappear from his own sight. He was still with himself, but he was in a very strange place.

For a second, everything had gone black. But then, just as suddenly, his eyes hurt from the golden glare that flared up about him. He put up a hand to his face and looked around.

The cubby had gone. He stood alone on a footpath, in the most beautiful place he had ever seen. When he looked in one direction, fields of golden green stretched out as far as he could see, until the land reached a dark high forest. When he looked in the other direction, just in front of his feet was the shore of a silver sea with the sun shining over it so that the waves sparkled like hundreds of tiny stars.

'Oh!' was all Rabbit could think to say.

His eyes soon became used to the bright light, and no longer hurt. He dropped his hand from his face and slipped the key into his pocket so that he wouldn't lose it. He waved his arms around in the lovely soft warm wind that was blowing – it filled him up like a balloon.

Then he sat down on a stone and had a bit of a think.

It's very nice here, thought Rabbit, much nicer than anywhere I've ever been, but what am I doing here?

Rabbit was small and used to not understanding what was going on, so it was not perhaps as much of a shock for him to find himself inside the Game of the Goose as it would be for someone older. And that is where he was – inside the Game.

He scratched his head. 'Number six,' he said to himself with a frown and nodded. Yes, that was the number he had thrown. Six. But now what? He felt cross, thinking of Fred and Rowley. Why hadn't they warned him, told him what was going to happen?

If I could swim, he thought, looking out at the water, that would be a very nice thing to do. But he couldn't swim.

The sea stretched far away. The little waves bobbed gently up and down.

'Oh!' said Rabbit again. 'What's that?'

Amongst the bobbing waves there seemed to be one that was larger and a different colour: white instead of blue. And it grew larger and whiter and seemed to be coming towards him.

'It's a sail boat!' cried Rabbit in excitement.

It was a red wooden boat with a white sail and nobody steering. Rabbit could hardly believe his luck. He loved sail boats! But he had never been near one in his life and had only seen them in pictures.

The boat came right up to the edge of the sea. Rabbit ran into the water, sinking in the sand. He kicked his sandals off. The water was as warm as a bath. When it was up to his knees, he reached the boat and threw his arms onto it to stop it from drifting away.

But the boat showed no signs of drifting away. It sat on the water, patiently waiting for him.

Can I? thought Rabbit.

He did not want to do anything that might get him into trouble. But he was so excited that he stopped thinking and pulled himself on board.

The boat was small, just big enough for Rabbit to stretch out his legs. As soon as he sat down, it began to move and the wind rose and filled the sails.

'This is wonderful!' shouted Rabbit to the sky.

Rabbit sailed off. He felt he was on the start of a great adventure. The warm water sprayed up on his face, his legs, as the boat gathered speed. How brave and free he was! He didn't feel like Rabbit at all.

The boat sailed right away from the shore into the middle of the sea. Now he couldn't see any land at all.

Perhaps I am in an ocean, he thought.

He leaned back in the gentle sunshine and peered over the edge. The water was clear and bright green, and he could see through it to coral and schools of tiny fish. He put his hand down and felt the little creatures pass through his fingers.

'That tickles!' he said in delight.

The boat slowed down, almost with a sigh. Rabbit stood up on the deck, steadying himself with his arms stretched wide like a tightrope walker. Then he lay on his stomach staring into the water and then on his back with his eyes closed. He let his hands and feet swing lazily over the edge as he drifted along.

For a long time he lay there, listening to the waves lapping, the sails squeaking and humming of the wind. He did not fall asleep but his mind became clear and soft as the sea. He forgot where he was. He forgot where he had come from. He forgot about his home and the cubby and Fred and Rowley and he forgot about the Game. It was as if he had never been born and this is where he had always been. Time disappeared.

But then suddenly Time returned. There was a cawing sound, louder than the lapping waves, and higher. Rabbit sat up.

It sounded like a distant sea bird. But as he scanned the sky he saw no sign of anything. He must have imagined it. And was he also imagining it, or had the sky grown a little darker? And the waves a little rougher? He felt a sudden panic. Rabbit wanted to stay happy, he did not want to be afraid.

The wind began to whistle, lowly, and was cold. The sun grew dim behind grey clouds. The waves swelled. Rabbit was afraid. He hung on tightly to the side of the boat, which was rising and falling steeply. What if he fell into the ocean and were drowned?

Lightning split the sky. Rabbit screamed. He wanted to cover his ears from the rolling thunder but he was frightened to let go of the sides of the little boat.

The boat rocked high and low, the sails ripped. Rabbit's fingers did not let go, he did not know he was so strong. He was wet through, his clothes were torn.

The sky and sea were black, the boat tossed violently. The sail twisted.

And then came a wave that was too big. Too big for Rabbit. It rose like a monster and spread its great arms above him and after a moment high in the air came crashing down on the terrified child and threw him off the boat and into the depths of angry water. Rabbit felt a great blow to his head, his mouth filled with water and he spun downwards.

· 8 ·

The Island of Children

'Look at him! He's so pale!'
'And look at his clothes – he's so torn up!'
'I wonder how long he's been lying here.'
'Can't be very long or he'd be dead.'
'Perhaps he is dead!'
'No, he's breathing. Can't you see?'
'Feel his skin, he's as cold as snow.'

A hand touched Rabbit's forehead and quickly lifted off again.

'He moved!'
'No!'
'I saw him – he moved. He's alive!'
'I told you he was.'
'Where did he come from?'
'I wonder if he can talk?'
'I wonder who he is?'

Rabbit opened his eyes. He shut them. Then, with a struggle, somehow he managed to open them again.

The little voices that had been piping about his aching head fell silent. Rabbit stared up. He moved his neck one way and then the other.

He was surrounded by children. Dozens of children stretching on up the beach into the bush.

He opened his mouth but he could not make any words.

That set the little voices off again.

'He's trying to say something!'

'Give him a drink of water.'

'He's hurt.'

'Poor thing, poor thing.'

'Look at his eyes! They're beautiful.'

'But he's frightened. Why is he frightened?'

One of the children knelt down next to him, her cupped hands filled with water which she sloshed over his face. Rabbit gulped and spluttered and sat up coughing, catching his breath.

'Oh!' gasped Rabbit.

'Now he looks better.'

'Now he's not going to die!'

'He looks lovely.'

'Wipe down his poor face.'

'Help him sit up.'

They surrounded him, helping him lean against

them. They stroked him and patted him like a little puppy. All the children were dressed in white tunics, like drooping sheets. Some of them were very dirty from mud and sand. They wore flowers around their necks, their waists, in their hair.

'He is lovely!'

'He will be my friend!'

'He will be a friend to all of us.'

'But he will like me the best.'

'No, he will like me the best.'

'He must be hungry, look how thin he is!'

'Are you hungry? Are you hungry?'

One of the children had suddenly thought to ask him directly. It gave him a shock. She knelt down and stared at him earnestly through her fringe of curling red hair.

'Yes,' said Rabbit, dazed.

The children leapt and cheered and hurried about to find food. The red-haired child stayed. She dug a pile of sand and propped him up against it. She covered his head with leaves to shade him from the sun.

'Do you feel better now?' she asked.

Rabbit nodded. But where was he? Was he still in the Game? And what had happened to his boat?

'My boat,' he said, 'I had a little boat . . .' And he trailed off with a terrible sadness. He'd had the boat for such a very short time, and he felt that he would never have it again.

'Did you fall off a boat? Is that how you got here?' said the kind child.

'There was a storm,' whispered Rabbit.

The child looked puzzled.

'It was awful,' said Rabbit, and he stopped. He remembered his little golden key – what if it had fallen into the water? But he reached into his pocket and there it was. He drew it out in relief, but also surprise. It had grown larger! As large as a real key!

'What's that?' asked the little girl.

'It's my key!' said Rabbit. 'I thought I might have lost it.'

The girl nodded thoughtfully. Then she said, 'I'll get you a piece of string – you can tie it around your neck.'

She jumped up and ran over to one of the palm trees that lined the beach, and she tore a thread from its trunk. She gave him the thread, which was strong and thick like raffia. She watched carefully as Rabbit threaded the key onto the string and then tied it around his neck.

'Thank you,' he said.

'Here are the others!' she cried, standing up. 'Now we can eat!'

Rabbit looked up. The children were tumbling down the sandbanks in a frenzy with armfuls of fruit.

Rabbit was starving.

'Look how he's smiling now!' laughed the child with the red curly hair.

Rabbit ate and drank. All sorts of strange and delicious things, things he had never tasted. The children also fell upon the food as though they too had not eaten in hours. They all ate together on the beach, like a glorious picnic as the sun set. Some of the children paddled in the water, some played games on the sand with balls.

Rabbit watched everything. He was too shy to play. He was amazed by these laughing, running children. Where were their parents? Where were their houses, and their beds?

The child with the red hair did not join in the games. She sat next to him, she was looking after him. Perhaps she knew how lonely he would feel if he sat by himself and watched.

'What's your name?' said Rabbit at last, because it would be nice to call her something.

The child smiled at him, but she didn't answer. Perhaps she didn't hear him. He asked again: 'What's your name?'

The child leant over him and brushed his hair back from his eyes.

'My name's Rabbit,' said Rabbit, persisting. Didn't she understand him? 'What's your name?'

She didn't understand. She kept smiling as though she just wanted to be happy, and she wanted him to be happy, too.

In fact, she didn't have a name. None of the children on that island had names, Rabbit realised after a while. They didn't call each other anything. They all just cried out to each other, to whoever was near.

Soon it became quite dark, and they lit torches with fire. A group of them came over, lifted Rabbit up, and carried him by torchlight up the beach, into the green darkness of a forest.

'You can sleep next to me,' said Rabbit's friend with the red hair.

So this is where they slept! In the flickering light, Rabbit saw the rows of little shallow holes in the ground, and the children lying down into them, falling silent suddenly, exhausted, like soldiers after a battle. The little girl curled up on the floor, and patted the ground next to her. Obediently, Rabbit lay down. The torches were put out and in an instant, all the children were asleep. All except Rabbit.

He stared at the girl with the curly red hair as she slept. Who was she, and where had she come from? Where had any of the children come from? Was this their life forever – was this his new life?

And what about the Game? Rabbit frowned. It was hard to remember the Game. It was hard even to remember the others, Fred and Rowley, although he felt they were there in his head, or at least someone was there.

Rabbit rolled onto his back and looked at the open sky. There were no stars at all, but there was a huge luminous beautiful moon, wide and yellow and still.

· 9 ·

Rowley's Turn

'Where's Rabbit?' said Rowley.

Rowley and Fred sat opposite each other in the dark, dank cubby-house. The place where Rabbit had been sitting was empty.

'Where'd he go?' said Rowley. 'He was just there.'

'And now he's gone.' Fred's voice trembled.

Rowley went to the door of the cubby. He looked up and down the hot expanse of yard that had once been three and now was one. There was no sign of Rabbit anywhere.

'He must have gone out while we weren't looking,' he said, turning back.

'We were looking,' said Fred.

Rowley repeated, 'It doesn't make sense. It doesn't make sense,' as though if he said it often enough, an understanding of what had happened to Rabbit would come over him.

'Are you going to keep playing or what?' snapped Fred. 'It's your turn.'

Rowley sat down again, but he felt a bit sick somewhere. Something wasn't right. Something big was not right. Where was Rabbit? But Rowley didn't know what else to do. Fred was breathing at him, like a dragon.

'All right,' he muttered.

Rowley rolled the die. Again it tumbled over and over like a clockwork toy. They both followed it with their eyes, hypnotised. At last it came to a halt.

'Another six,' said Rowley. 'We're lucky today.'

And he picked up the pair of tiny winged shoes and moved them from the square marked START into Path Number Two.

· *10* ·

Wings

For a moment, everything went black, as it had for Rabbit. Then, just as quickly, it was as bright as fire and Rowley shaded his eyes from the glare.

Rowley was older than Rabbit – Rowley did not accept all that came his way with quite Rabbit's simplicity.

What's this? he thought roughly.

Rowley looked carefully around him. There were trees and flowers, and a kind of lake-like expanse in the distance, and dark mountains surrounded by forests. It didn't look at all real to him, but like a mirage in the desert that would disappear, or turn into something bad and black.

Where was Rabbit? He must be somewhere near by. Probably hiding, he was such a scared sort of thing.

'Rabbit!' he called out, and again louder, 'It's me, Rowley! Come out!'

Nothing. It was as still as a painting.

Rowley did not find it beautiful as Rabbit had. It was hot and strange and rich. He did not belong here – soon someone would tell him that. Rowley felt angry. He felt himself tense up, as though someone were about to pummel him.

'I'm in the Game,' he said out loud, although he could not believe it.

He knew he wasn't dreaming or imagining it. Rowley knew exactly what real felt like, and this was real. He was in the Game, on Path Number Two, just as he had chosen back in the cubby. How am I going to get out of here? he thought, and he bit his lip very hard. He didn't want to burst into tears, or to panic. He had to be strong, he told himself.

'I have had some bad times before,' he said, 'and I can be strong.'

Rowley had had bad times, although he was not very old. Some of the bad things had happened inside his head, and some of them outside. But he was strong.

To his horror, he found that his eyes were filling with tears.

'NO!' cried Rowley, angry.

He stamped his feet. As he did so, he felt something move. He jumped. Was it a snake?

'Hey!'

It wasn't a snake. Amazed, he saw that his feet were clothed in silver shoes, with silver wings on the heels. The charm, his counter, had magically grown and flown down to his own feet!

The little wings on his heels were flapping together madly. They were trying to fly away. But how could they lift something so heavy? Rowley was big for his age – he could punch hard and kick high. He laughed at the wings, flapping like that!

At that moment, the ground gave way beneath him.

'Oh!' Rowley gasped. The wings were pulling him up into the air! First just a little bit, then a bit more, then he was about the height of a daisy bush!

'This is – it's –'

He almost overbalanced, but managed to straighten himself up, rather like being on roller-skates. That gave him an idea – he pushed his feet gingerly forward one by one into the air, like skating. Then his whole body followed and he began to glide.

'Oh!' cried Rowley again. This time he really did forget all about being angry and frightened because the moment a person learns to fly, everything else they ever felt in their whole life just vanishes and all that's left is the wonder of it.

He skimmed quickly along, just above the surface

of the earth, faster than anyone could run – and so smooth, and the wind rushed over him like warm water. He sped around in circles and up and down by pointing his heels in different directions. When he wanted to stay still and catch his breath, he moved his feet together from side to side and hovered.

'I can do anything! I can go anywhere!' he shouted. 'I can win the Game!'

He bounded through the air like a giant. But perhaps a little too quickly, because suddenly he tumbled backwards, rolling over in somersaults, just managing to miss cracking his head on the ground. Then he was tangled up somehow, in a net that felt as though it were full of fish hooks that bit into his skin and caught on his hair. He tried to shake it off, and became even more entangled.

'What is this!' he muttered.

He stopped thrashing about and looked at what had caught him. It wasn't a net, it was a thorny bush.

'A rose bush!' said Rowley in disgust, not being especially fond of flowers.

The leaves were dark green and shiny like holly, with hundreds of little crimson buds scattered about. He began to untangle himself, pulling the thorns from his clothes.

It was only when he was standing up, free of the bush, that he had a good look at where he now was.

In front of him was a high winding wall that stretched off into a curving distance.

'It looks like the walls of an old city,' he said, in surprise.

Rowley had seen pictures of old cities in history books. These were cities from hundreds, even thousands of years ago, surrounded by stone walls to keep out the enemies. Soldiers would stand with bows and arrows on the top of the wall.

But there were no soldiers guarding this city. Rowley stepped forward, keeping his feet hard on the ground – he did not want to go up in the air just then, not till he had had a good look.

The wall was deserted but he could just see in part of it an open stone gateway. Coming out of it was the faintest cloud of white dust. Should he go in?

'It's an adventure,' Rowley told himself firmly.

Holding his chin up and shuffling along the sandy ground to stop himself from shooting upwards, Rowley made his way to the city wall. Although it had looked far off, he seemed to reach it quite quickly, more quickly than he would have liked. The cloud that had been so faint became thick and white and was rolling out of the entrance like steam from a huge kettle.

Rowley raised the sleeve of his shirt to cover his mouth, as he had seen firemen do on television.

'Here goes,' he said.

And he raised his feet in the air, and flew into the gate of the old city.

The Old City

The dust rose thickly about him. He was choking in a kind of dirty, spinning fog. He could see nothing but dust. It entered his eyes, his throat. It was so thick the little wings on his shoes could scarcely keep beating.

I must get some shelter! he thought.

He beat his arms in the air, trying to make some space for himself. The dust storm, if that is what it was, made a high whining sound that rang in his ears.

'Help!' he shouted as loudly as he could.

There must be somebody there, he thought. Inside a city wall must be a city. In a city there must be people.

'Help!' he screamed out again, but his mouth filled with dust and he coughed and stumbled.

He heard a voice. 'Over here!'

Rowley twirled around.

'Over here! Come on!'

Rowley put his head down and stumbled, half running, half flying in the direction of the voice. He had no idea what was in front or behind him – he might have been going headlong into a wall, but he didn't care. He followed the voice, and tripped into a doorway and onto a hard floor.

'Ah!' said the voice.

Rowley opened his eyes. The first thing he noticed was that there was no dust. He was in some kind of stone room, an alcove built back from the street. The clouds of dust rolled by outside in a whirlwind, but did not come in. He sat there, breathing heavily.

'You're here!' said the voice.

Wiping dirt from his face, Rowley looked up to see who was speaking. It was a knight! A knight in armour! Just like in a book.

At least Rowley supposed it was a knight inside the armour, because armour was all he could see. The metal face mask was pulled down, and the knight had metal gloves and shoes, so there was no skin visible anywhere.

The knight held out a gloved hand and pulled Rowley, coughing again, to his feet.

'Thanks,' Rowley said hoarsely. 'I'm Rowley.'

'And I'm the Last Crusader,' replied the knight solemnly.

Rowley took in some more deep breaths.

'Don't you have a name?' he asked.

'No name,' the knight replied, peculiarly both mournful and proud. 'Only a title.'

The storm was making a dreadful dry wailing sound. Rowley winced.

'When will it stop?' he asked the knight, pointing outside.

The knight clanked, shifting his arms and legs as though they were stiff with age.

'I am so glad you are here at last,' was all he said. 'How long I have been waiting! Even at my age, to wait is difficult.'

'Oh,' said Rowley. He paused. 'Waiting for what?'

'For you!' The knight's mask moved slowly up and down in a nod.

Rowley hardly knew what to think. How could the knight have been waiting for him? Then, because he couldn't think of anything else, he asked, 'How long have you been waiting?'

'Oh, centuries,' replied the knight.

Rowley had no answer. In a strange sort of way it seemed to make sense that the knight had been waiting for him for centuries.

'I should feel funnier,' he said to himself, 'but I can't. It's rather like,' and he stopped. 'It's rather like reading a book. You just somehow disappear into it for a while. The old world will come back, but just now it's so far away. I can hardly remember it.'

Rowley looked about him again, at the stone room.

'Where are we?' he asked.

'We are in the Game,' replied the knight simply.

Well, he knew that already. 'Are you –' began Rowley uncertainly. 'Are you – do you – I mean –'

Was the knight actually playing the Game? Or did he belong to the Game? Why did he sound so sad?

'You have just begun the Game, haven't you, Rowley,' said the knight. 'You are young and full of energy and need to play. But I am old. I am very old.'

Rowley shivered. Had the knight once been young and grown old and lonely in this place?

'There was a group of us playing the Game, you know,' continued the knight, as though answering Rowley's unspoken question. 'We were all in the Game together. Now I am the only one left.'

'What happened to the others?' said Rowley.

'Gone,' said the knight. 'All gone.'

Rowley didn't like the sound of that. 'But –' he frowned. 'What happened? I mean – did they win?'

'Win?' The knight's voice was thoughtful. 'I don't know about win. To be honest, I don't know if this is a game that you can win.'

'That's what a game is. It's like a race. Somebody wins,' objected Rowley.

'Is it?' replied the knight.

Rowley didn't know how to answer that – well, not politely. If the poor old knight didn't know, well . . .

Suddenly there was a hush. The wind, thought Rowley, the wind is leaving. He pulled himself over to the door and looked out. It was true, the storm was dying, the dust settling. He could see into the empty laneways of the old city, into the mass of ancient buildings with narrow slits for windows, separated by alleys winding steeply downwards.

The knight creaked onto his legs, leaning against Rowley, looking out. The dust clouds now were low as though people and carts and donkeys were tramping up and down. But there were no people. The only signs of recent life were the dead leaves scattered on the doorsteps.

'So,' cried the knight, standing straight and tall, 'are you ready?'

'Ready?'

'Yes,' said the knight. 'I need you to lead me out of here.'

'Me?'

'Yes, you,' said the knight. 'If I can only get out of this old city, I'm sure I can find my friends, my knights!'

'But – you can just go out the gate,' said Rowley, bewildered. 'The way I came in. You don't need me!' He turned and pointed in the direction he had come. He stared open-mouthed, and his arm fell to his side. The gateway was gone! Only the wall remained.

'Rowley,' the knight sighed, shaking his metal head. 'You can never go out the way you came in.'

'Then how –' said Rowley. What was he going to do? How would he get out?

'You can help me, Rowley,' said the knight. 'I am old and almost blind. I will never get out of here without you.'

But the Game! Rowley wanted to win the Game, he wanted to beat Fred. He wasn't worried about Rabbit, of course he would beat Rabbit. But Fred – he couldn't bear it if she won.

'But –' he said again. He felt the knight's blind eyes staring at him intently. Thoughts entered his head on wings of their own. Perhaps he could just slip away. There was no one else who would know. The old city was deserted. The little wings would scarcely make a sound as they carried him off, and then he could escape from this dreadful place – get back into the Game. It wasn't fair – how could the old knight expect him to . . .

The knight leaned forward and laid his heavy arm on Rowley's shoulder. Rowley staggered under the sudden weight. There was no more space for thoughts. The knight was old and weak, Rowley was young and fierce and brave. He would have to lead him out.

And just then, Rowley heard a flapping noise, as though something had swept past him, but when he turned to look there was nothing there.

· 12 ·

Fred Alone

Fred stood alone in front of the Game of the Goose. Rabbit first, and now Rowley. Two living breathing blood-filled boys. Both of them, gone.

'Well,' she said to no one. 'Now it's my turn.'

She stared down at the board, at the paths taken by Rabbit and Rowley. She picked up the die – it was cold and heavy. She took a deep breath. Then she let it drop.

Just as had happened with both Rabbit and Rowley, the die rolled in circles around the entire board. Finally it came to a stop.

It was a four. Fred licked her lips. She picked up her piece, the girdle, and prepared herself to disappear, just as the others had done. She stayed her hand a moment above Path Number Three.

'Here goes!' said Fred, and put the charm on the path.

She counted four spaces. 'One, two, three, four.'
Nothing happened.

Fred sat and waited. And nothing happened.

She picked up the die and threw it again. And again she waited.

Fred did not know how long she waited. She was not usually patient, in fact she was a rather angry, jumping about sort of person, but this time she sat still as ice.

She twisted her head – what was that breathing sound? Was someone in the cubby with her? But of course no one was, it was only Jemima Puddleduck, who lay asleep with her furry chest rising up and down like a bellows, her eyes closed.

Well, if that wasn't proof that something was seriously wrong, nothing was. What was it that Rowley had said – she was a Restless Cavy, an animal that never slept.

Fred walked out of the cubby into the sunshine, up the back steps, inside the house. It was empty. Her mother must be lying down. She went into her mother's bedroom and sure enough, the blinds were down and there was her mother in the daytime dark on the bed, in a deep sleep, just like Jemima. Her skin was so white. Fred leant over her, wanting to wake her but somehow unable to. She seemed so very far away, even though she was right there in front of her.

Fred laid her head on the bedside table, her cheek resting against the cool wood. 'I feel sick,' she said. She put a hand to her forehead – she was very hot – she must have a temperature. Maybe that's what was wrong.

Because everything was wrong. Why didn't the Game work for her? Why was no one around – why didn't Rabbit's mother come over and ask where he was? Or Rowley's? Why was her own mother asleep? Perhaps she was sick; sleeping sickness, she had heard of that – when people just suddenly fell asleep and never woke up.

Well, I must keep awake then, Fred thought.

She stood up and stamped her feet. She must stay alert. She jumped up and down on the spot. She ran out to the kitchen and splashed water over her face, wetting her hair and her clothes. She slapped her own cheeks.

'Right,' she said aloud. 'Right.'

She walked briskly out of the kitchen into the back-yard, the screen door banging like a drum-roll behind her. She marched down into the cubby-house. The candle was still burning. She knelt down in front of the Game.

'I am going to get into this Game,' she said with as much resolve as she had ever had.

She gazed down at it: the winding paths, the dark cryptic writing. The board was worn and faded, but still so – so beautiful, thought Fred wistfully. She wondered how old it really was – and how many people had played it before. It looked as though it might be hundreds of years old. It should be in a museum, in a glass case. People should have to pay money to see it and file past one by one, like looking at the dead body of a great hero. Yet here it was before her, in her own hands.

She looked at the goose, its golden wings and its enigmatic face, and the motto that Rabbit had asked her about – *The Race is Not Always to the Swift, Nor the Battle to the Strong.* Now she noticed, just underneath it, something more in that black twisted writing that she had not seen before. Straining in the dark, she read:

But Whoever Hopes the Most –

Then it stopped. The writing seemed to sway and disappear into the dust. Her eyes slid further down onto the board, and she saw . . .

'Don't be silly,' she said at once. 'It must be the flickering of the candle flame.'

But it wasn't. There were people moving there! Tiny people. She screwed up her eyes. The little figures seemed to be in some kind of maze – two of them. She looked closer. It couldn't be –

'Rowley,' Fred breathed.

Who was the other person? Fred wondered – she

couldn't make it out. It definitely wasn't Rabbit. It was far too big. Where was Rabbit?

As though in answer to her question, Fred's eyes slid again further across the board and there was Rabbit, sitting by himself at the water's edge.

'Oh!' said Fred.

How alone he looked, and little! How – how – imprisoned, she thought, although he sat under the open sky. She remembered the Noah's Ark and something inside her cracked.

'Oh Rabbit!' she whispered. 'I wish . . .'

Fred closed her eyes. Twice she had tried to get into the Game and failed. But maybe the third time?

But Whoever Hopes the Most . . .

She raised the die above her head. She hoped. 'Please,' she said out loud.

Fred dropped the die onto the board. The flame of the candle burned blue. There was a rustle of wind. The die rolled. It came to a halt, finally, on the six.

Fred gasped. She felt as though she were being borne up into the air in a soft rush of wings.

She was in the Game of the Goose.

· 13 ·

The Whispering Market

Like Rabbit and Rowley before her, the first thing Fred was aware of was darkness and then a bright light. But when that died away, she did not find herself, like them, alone in a solitary place. She was surrounded by people in bright robes, and carts and animals – donkeys and camels and cats – so many cats, scurrying about her feet; on tables, kittens perched on people's shoulders, hanging on with their claws.

As she looked around in amazement, Fred realised that she had arrived right in the middle of a market, although what exactly was being bought and sold was difficult to say. Was it jewels, grains, cheeses? Every time Fred swung her head around things jostled up and down in a blur. People pushed her from in front and behind.

And the noise! Not the normal sort of busy market

noise – it was a peculiar hissing, as though everyone in the market had been told to keep their voices down. Everyone was whispering and hundreds of people urgently whispering is not quiet at all – it was like listening to a sea-shell magnified a thousand times. Even the cats were whispering.

There was no shelter above the stalls from the sun which seemed very low and large and almost orange. Fred wiped the sweat from her forehead, perspiration dripped into her eyes. The market was jam-packed and any forward or backward movement was terribly slow.

Am I really in the Game? thought Fred.

This was not somehow what she had imagined, although she would not have been able to say just what she *had* imagined. She had only known that she had wanted to be there, more than anything. And now she was.

'Would you like to buy?' whispered someone next to her, right in her ear, making her start in fright.

'Look here!' whispered someone else on her other side, and then behind and in front.

'Would you like to buy? Look here!'

Fred turned here and there and looked but still she couldn't understand what was being sold. As soon as she turned, the person selling had disappeared and gone on to sell to someone else – no one stayed for more than a moment before losing interest.

I have to get out of here, thought Fred.

The crowd was as thick as a wall. She would have to push her way through. She raised her elbows in the air.

'Excuse me,' she said to whoever was in front of her.

As the words came out of her mouth, all the whispering stopped at once, and became a single horrified gasp. Fred knew a disaster was about to happen, and what's more, it was about to happen to her. The gaze of the crowd was upon her, rows of large round bright blue eyes still and cold as marbles.

Somebody whispered, 'She spoke!'

And there was a horrible whispering echo that spun through the crowd. 'She spoke, she spoke, she spoke, she spoke, shespoke, shespoke, shpoke, shpoke, sshpoke . . .'

On and on – Fred thought her head would split in two. As she put her hands to her ears, she was seized upon by dozens of pairs of hands, dragging her this way and that, no one seemed to know where. Things tumbled about on high, underfoot, stalls crashed and wood split, metal clanged. Fred was carried roughly into the whispering air – she kicked out and threw her arms up, her fists punching and she shouted out as loudly as she could, 'Let me go!'

Then her mouth was covered by hundreds of

hands. She bit and spat, but she was overpowered. Hands covered her eyes. She could see nothing, nothing to tell how fast or slow she was going or where she was going to.

Then just as suddenly as it had started, the arms holding her let go and she was falling down slippery steps into darkness. A great door swung shut with a creak and a bolt was drawn across it with a final thud.

· 14 ·

The Maze of Despair

owley and the knight stepped out of the cool
stone room onto the street, the knight leaning
heavily. It felt to Rowley as though he were almost
carrying him. His own winged feet were of no use to
him at all.

Slowly, they trod through the empty lanes of the
old city. The only sounds were the squeaking of
the knight's crumbling armour and the fall and shuffle
of their feet on the pavement. There was nobody else
there, not even a mouse. The city was empty with
death. But not even with death, thought Rowley. It
felt like a place where no one had ever lived at all.

We are the only live people who have ever been
here, he thought.

The lanes became narrower and the buildings
turned into walls. Gradually, Rowley realised that the

old city was disappearing. There were no more windows, no more doorways. It became so steep and dark and winding, both Rowley and the knight clung to each other to stop themselves from falling forward.

Neither of them spoke. Rowley's shoulders ached, his throat was dry. The pathway twisted in a spiral. Rowley and the knight edged forward, then came face to face with a brick wall.

'Not a dead end!' Rowley groaned.

There was nothing for it but to go back the way they had come, but the path was so narrow they had to go backwards which was even slower. When at last the walls stopped turning and they returned to the beginning of the spiral, Rowley saw that the path forked in two. There had been two ways to go and he had taken the wrong one.

'Where are we?' he frowned.

He put his fingers to the walls that surrounded them. They were rough and cold.

It's a maze, he thought, in a rush of understanding.

The streets of the old city had turned into a maze. But it was not at all a friendly sort of maze as you might see in a picture book or at a fun fair. It was ancient and full of malice. Rowley was afraid.

He gave his shoulder a shake. He remembered what he had read about mazes in books. There were rules to solve them, to find your way. When there was a choice of paths, you always took the same direction, the right or the left. Then you would get out.

So which way? There was no point asking the knight for help. He couldn't see, he could hardly walk.

The other path was hopeless, thought Rowley, so we better go this way.

To his relief, this new way was much straighter and the walk easier. The knight's breathing grew softer, and in the same rhythm as Rowley's.

This is all right, thought Rowley. We'll be getting somewhere soon.

Then suddenly the path veered to the left and then again to the right.

'What's this?' said Rowley.

One more turn, and another, and they came to another fork in the path.

'Wait a minute,' said Rowley. 'We've been here before . . .'

Had they? It looked the same.

'I don't want to go down that spiral again,' he said to himself. 'But what's the point of just going back on the same path?'

Perhaps it wasn't the same. It couldn't be – they had come so far. Surely they were getting somewhere!

'It looks like there's a choice,' he muttered, 'but there's not.'

Rowley felt sick and angry. He knew what had happened. They were lost. They were lost in a deep way. Whenever he had been lost before, in his other life, before the Game, he had always known that it would only last for a little while, that somehow he would find where it was he had to go, he would see something he recognised, or someone would appear to help him.

But in this dark maze with the knight, he felt there was no way out, and there never would be. The rules didn't work here. This was a cruel and dark and pitiless place and it wanted him to be lost for ever.

'What are we going to do?' he cried out loud.

He looked at the winged shoes on his feet, black with dust and soot. What a pity he couldn't use them now and fly away – how wonderful it had been to fly! But he would never fly again.

Suddenly, the knight spoke. It had been so long since he had heard his voice, Rowley was startled, as though the walls were speaking.

'Let's sit for a while, Rowley,' said the knight. 'You are tired. Let's rest. I have waited so long, I can wait a little longer.'

Slowly, he lowered himself down to the floor. He stretched out his heavy legs so that they crossed the pathway.

'It's all right,' he said, reading Rowley's thoughts.

'No one will pass by us here. No one will ever pass us by.'

The way the knight spoke, it was as though he were giving Rowley comfort. But despair wrapped itself around him at the thought of such terrible loneliness. He sank down on his knees next to the knight, covering his face with his hands.

· 15 ·

Panic

Rabbit had woken up feeling uncomfortable. He was not usually very keen on having baths, but that was the first thought that entered his head – it would be lovely to lie in a warm soapy bath!

He stood up, under a canopy of trees. The sun was high in the sky. What on earth was he doing here? He couldn't remember – anything.

'I am only six,' said Rabbit to himself. 'That is not many years. I should be able to remember everything. Imagine if I was sixty!'

He looked around. It was a grassy leafy shady sort of place, a kind of wood or forest. He could not remember ever having been here before.

Oh well, thought Rabbit sensibly, I'm here now. It won't help knowing where I was before.

His legs felt sore, as though he had been running

for a long time. And he was thirsty.

'I suppose,' said Rabbit out loud, 'I might as well walk somewhere and perhaps I will find some water.'

He started walking through the woods, pushing aside the flowers that hung from the branches. He didn't have to walk for long, because there was water everywhere in the Game of the Goose. He came out from the thickness of the trees to an open place where a small pretty green fountain was bubbling away. Rabbit knelt down and put his face right into it and shook his head from side to side like a dog.

When he came up for air the pretty water was inky with soot. Rabbit rubbed his hands together in it and it became inkier still.

My face is so dirty! he wondered. Have I been in a fire?

He sat cross-legged next to the fountain and made himself think really hard. But there was nothing in his head apart from himself.

'Just my own self,' he said.

He did not mind being by his own self. He was used to it. It was peaceful. He sat for a while, cool and fresh, listening to the sounds of the trees and the insects and the birds. Especially the birds. There was a great twittering of birds coming from somewhere near by, but that he could not see.

There must be a whole flock of them, he thought,

and he got up to have a look. He was curious. Would they be the same kinds of birds as the ones in the trees at home?

He followed the sound through shaded bushes. Everything smelt green, like cut grass. As he grew closer, not only did the twittering become louder but it seemed to sound like laughter and chattering. Could it be people, not birds?

He pushed back a long ferny fringe, like thrusting open a door, onto more deep green darkness. There was a gust of wind and the noise of flight and feathers floating in the air. Rabbit blinked.

He heard something crack behind him – or was it in front? He trod forward hesitantly.

'Hallo!'

No answer. He stepped forward again. A moment ago he had been happy by himself, but now his heart was beating fast.

'Hallo!' He put his hand up to the key hanging around his neck. 'Hallo?'

At last someone said, 'Are you all right?'

Rabbit swung around. There was nobody.

'Up here!'

He looked up. It was the girl with red hair, slung over the branch of a tree of yellow flowers!

'Oh!' he cried. 'I'm so glad to see you!'

The girl jumped down onto the grass next to him.

'That's good,' she said. 'Are you all right? You look upset. Did something happen to you?'

Rabbit didn't know.

'I – it's –' he said, stumbling on his words. 'It's – I, I don't know.'

Then, quite unexpectedly, he said, 'I think I want to go home.'

'Home,' said the girl, smiling. 'You are home. This is home.'

'But –' Rabbit shook his head. 'Do I live here now?'

'Where else would you live?' replied the girl.

Rabbit stared. 'I'm not sure,' he said. 'Home . . .'

Rabbit tried to think. His mind felt empty, like an old carton, like a hollow tree. Home. He searched through the shadows. He could remember what the Game looked like, that was all. The Game, the box, the pieces.

Again he put his hand around the key. The girl watched him.

'You can throw that away now,' she said in a casual way. 'You won't need it any more. Now that you're with us.'

Rabbit did not reply. It didn't seem right to throw away a key. It must lock something, or unlock it, even if he didn't know what it was. Someone might need it.

'You can give it to me, if you like,' the girl said.

She held out her hand. Rabbit was naturally obedient. If someone asked him for something, it was his nature to give it, even if he didn't want to. But perhaps he remembered more than he knew of his life before the Game, because even while he was taking the string uncertainly from his neck, quite suddenly he changed his mind.

'I want to keep it,' he said, and a small stubborn look came into his eyes. 'And I want to go home.'

The girl shrugged and turned a circle on her foot. Then she turned another circle and danced about in front of him, like a little ballerina in a music box.

She pointed to a path through the trees.

'If you really want to leave,' she said, 'there's a bridge. I could show you, if you like. Not now, but later.'

'What bridge?' asked Rabbit.

'The Golden Bridge,' she said. 'That's the only way off the island. You can come by boat, but you can only leave by foot.'

'Oh!' said Rabbit.

'I can show you,' said the girl again, reaching out her small hand to his. 'The others are playing down on the beach. Why don't you come and play with us?'

Rabbit smiled at her. How nice she was, and kind to him. He could hear that strange twittering laughter, and the sound of a ball being hit up into the air.

'All right,' he said, and took her hand and they walked together towards the shore.

· 16 ·

The Cold Tower

Fred lay motionless where she had fallen. She blinked. She breathed in and out through her nose. The air smelt of moss.

She lifted herself up on her sore arms. She looked around her. Wet stone. And very cold.

'I'm in prison,' she said out loud.

This was bad. This was not what she had hoped for but oddly enough, she felt quite calm.

Well, it's happened now, she thought. It's not fair, but it's happened.

It wasn't fair – just because she forgot to whisper – why, nobody actually told her it was forbidden so dreadfully to speak. Just because everybody else was whispering, why should she?

I'm glad I spoke out loud, she thought. What a silly rule. All that whispering, it's just ridiculous. She felt rather pleased with herself.

Fred stood up and walked about the cell. She couldn't believe it but she had no choice – the long flight of steps down which she had been thrown had vanished. There were no stairs and, what's more, there was no door.

Now Fred was in almost every respect a practical person. 'I can see quite clearly,' she said firmly. 'So there must be a window somewhere, or a light.'

She looked all over the walls. Somewhere there must be a brick missing or a crack letting the light in. But the walls were as neat and tight as a prison should be. Then she looked up at the ceiling.

'Oh!' said Fred, her neck leaning right back.

There was something up there! A small square of light. But so high up.

'Well,' said Fred. 'At least it's there. And that's how I'll get out of here.'

She gazed at the square of light – such a perfect square, it must be a window of some kind. The light streamed down from it in a beam and then dispersed into the darkness of the cell. Fred shivered to think of the horrible blackness she would be trapped in without it. What if, like the stairway, this little window should also disappear? Then she would just die; slowly freeze away to nothing.

Right, she thought, I've got to get up there. I've got

to. She paced up and down the tiny floor. She felt in her pockets – empty. But – there was something hanging from her waist.

'What –'

Fred drew it out – it was a gleaming silver dagger! 'It's my charm,' she said in wonder. 'But it's become big!'

She held it up in front of her face – it was as sharp as a razor-blade and shining like a river. Fred looked down again at her waist – tied around it was a thick silver braid. She drew her fingers along the smoothness of the silver belt. It was the most beautiful thing she had ever owned in her life.

Her dagger was so sharp, perhaps she could drive it into the stone and get a foothold somehow . . .

If I could . . . she thought, becoming excited.

She untied the silver girdle from her waist. It was long, like the scarf of a magician, and at least as tall as she was, perhaps twice so.

'If I . . .' she said.

She tied one end of the girdle around the hilt of her dagger as tightly as she could, with three, four, five knots. She tied a loop in the other end, which she slipped over her left hand. Then with her right hand, and summoning every cell of strength, she threw the dagger up into the air so that it fell against the crumbling wall.

'Oh!' cried Fred.

It was magic! It was more magic than ordinary magic, because it did not need three times to make it happen. It was as if the wall were butter – the dagger slid into it and caught hold fast. Fred did not stop to think of what could go wrong. She had to move quickly or she would lose whatever she had gained. Holding the loop tightly, she pulled herself up the wall, pushing against it with her feet, scrambling up like an insect.

When she reached the dagger, she perched on bits of uneven stone, dug her fingers in, and clung there.

'I will hang on,' she told herself, 'or I will die in this place.'

The words seemed to lend her an extra force, and she said them again. 'I will hang on, or I will die in this place. I will hang on or I will die in this place.'

Clinging with her feet and one hand, she extracted the dagger and again threw it violently into the air – and again wonderfully, it slid into the wall way above her, and the climb continued.

Fred made her way towards the square of light, borne up by the girdle and the dagger. She did not count how many times she withdrew the dagger and threw it again. I will hang on or I will die in this place – this was the only thought she allowed herself.

That, and the awareness that the window was getting closer with every throw.

At last, Fred reached the moment of the final throw of the dagger. The window was right before her – with no bars, no glass, nothing, just a space into sunshine and warm drifting air. All she had to do was throw one last time and pull herself into the world, wherever and whatever it was.

'What's out there? What will happen to me when I get out? What if it doesn't catch hold?'

She glanced back down at the tower stretching under her, it seemed forever and she felt a kind of giddy terror.

Fred took a deep breath. She hurled the dagger into the open sky.

· 17 ·

The Peacock Forest

Fred came flying out of the dark tower with a bang and a roll and a bump.

'Oh!' she cried. 'I did it!'

She had done it! She was not dead, she was not even hurt. Her arm muscles were a little sore, that was all. She sat up on the soft grassy floor. She felt as though she were about to laugh.

I suppose I'm shocked or something, she thought, like people are after an accident.

Looking around, she caught sight of the dagger where it had landed deep in the trunk of a tree, the girdle lying beside it. She crawled over to it and tugged at the dagger to get it out, but it had stuck fast.

Did I throw it so hard? she wondered. She tugged a few more times, but it wouldn't loosen at all. Oh well, she thought, it's really the girdle I love the most, anyway.

She untied the silver braid from the handle of the dagger, and slipped it back around her waist. She took a few steps around the tree. Next to it was another, and another and another.

'It's like a forest of Christmas trees!' she said out loud.

It was quiet and brooding. Fred forgot she was tired.

Here I am, she thought as she went deeper into the forest.

After a while, she realised that she was not alone. In and out amongst the shadows of the tall trees were bobbing birds like large hens. There were several of them, treading through the fallen branches with long feet. Fred stood still for a moment and looked more carefully.

'They're peacocks!'

One of the birds stopped and turned its neck around, spreading its tail feathers out.

Fred was enchanted. She ran towards it to see it more clearly, but as she did so, it began to run away from her. Four, five, six other peacocks ran alongside it, their tail feathers sparkling like hundreds of smooth precious stones floating in the dark air.

Fred quickened her pace. So did the birds. Soon

they were all running together through the forest, as if they were being chased. Fred was panting, she wanted to stop, but she did not want to lose sight of the peacocks. Could peacocks fly? Fred wasn't sure – but they had wings. Could an animal have wings and not be able to fly? How terrible, she thought, even as she ran, to have something and to yearn for something and not be able to do it.

'Oh wait!' she cried out. 'Please wait!'

The trees had become very thick, a wall of wooden trunks. The peacocks slowed down. So did Fred. She took some deep breaths. Something had changed.

It's still a forest, she thought. But it's somewhere else as well.

The peacocks were now treading slowly and their heads turning this way and that as though they were cautiously listening for something. Their eyes gleamed, their wonderful feathers shone. Fred listened too – it was an echoey sound, like in a cave.

Above them it was night, starless but with a huge orange moon, shedding a weird glow all about her. Fred felt uncanny, she wanted to turn around and go back to where she had come from.

The peacocks had stopped. They were standing in a row. Fred stepped towards them, expecting them to run off again, but they didn't. She walked right up to them, their tail feathers trembling in the moonlight. When she reached them, they parted, three on each side.

'Oh!' said Fred, amazed.

It was Rowley and the old knight.

· 18 ·

The Waters of Forgetfulness

Rowley and Fred stared at each other like ghosts. 'It's you!' said Fred.

But there was something about him that seemed different – his face, his eyes. She couldn't work it out. Something had happened to him.

He was sitting on the ground, as she had seen him when she looked into the Game back in the cubbyhouse. Next to him was the knight.

A knight in shining armour, thought Fred, only more rusted than shining.

'Rowley?' she said, hesitantly.

He didn't reply. Didn't he recognise her?

'Our paths must have crossed,' she said.

Rowley looked up dully. He was holding the knight's helmeted head up against his shoulder.

'Rowley?' she said. 'It's me, Fred.'

Still he said nothing.

'Who's this?' asked Fred, pointing at the armour.

Rowley spoke, in such a low voice, not like him at all. 'It's – it's a friend of mine,' he said. 'He can't walk – he's so weak.'

Was Rowley crying? wondered Fred, shocked.

'What's wrong with him?' she said, practically.

'We're lost!' Rowley blurted out. 'It's a maze, can't you see! We're lost in a maze, and we'll never get back, ever! We're going to die here!'

Fred frowned. There really was something wrong with Rowley.

'It's not a maze,' she said, waving her arms around to show him. 'It's a forest.'

But Rowley's face was turned down at the ground. She gave him a little punch.

'It's a forest, Rowley. We're not lost. The peacocks led me here. They'll lead us out. We're all right. Look! Rowley.'

Perhaps this is what happens, she thought suddenly, when the paths cross. Maybe he was lost in a maze, but now it's changed, because I'm here.

'So we can go,' she said. 'We can keep playing the Game.'

She yanked Rowley's shirt. 'Come on, Rowley!'

Rowley shook his head. 'I can't,' he said. 'My friend can't move. He's too weak. And I can't leave him now.'

A peacock nudged Fred's leg. The bird turned its head, as though showing Fred something. Fred looked in the bird's direction.

It was a well! An old-fashioned well with a rounded roof, hidden in a grove of trees.

Fred thought quickly. 'I'll get your friend a drink of water, that'll give him a bit of strength!'

She didn't wait for Rowley to answer. She ran over to it. She had never used a well in her life, but there was a handle. All she had to do was turn it, surely.

But while she found a bucket hooked to the roof, where there should have been a rope to let it down into the water there was nothing. At least almost nothing, just the remains of what may have once been a rope that crumbled into the air even as she touched it.

'Oh!' Fred bit her lip.

She looked around, hands on her hips.

Of course! she thought, inspired. My girdle.

She pulled it from her waist and tied one end to the handle of the bucket.

Will it be long enough? she wondered, staring down into the black water, which seemed very far away.

She lowered the bucket down – it took a long time. The well was very deep. At last she heard a splash. She felt the bucket sink and become heavy.

'Now!' she said. 'The hard part.'

She hung onto the end of the girdle with both

arms, using all her strength. She pulled the bucket back up, it seemed to her, from the centre of the world. And in the same way it had magically lengthened, now the girdle became short again each time she pulled and the bucket lifted into the air.

At last she pulled it right out of the well, water spilling from side to side.

'There!' she said.

She rested the bucket on the wall of the well, while she raised a hand to her forehead and blew air from her mouth up to cool her face.

In that moment, the silver girdle slipped from the handle of the bucket. Like a snake, the knot untied itself and it slid soundlessly away, falling down into the well.

But, mysteriously, Fred noticed nothing. She did not even hear the tiniest splash as it reached the water. With the bucket in her hand, she'd already forgotten about it.

Very carefully, she carried the bucket over to where the knight half sat, half lay.

She knelt down next to Rowley. The knight's head rested on his shoulder. Feeling rather silly, Fred spoke into the mask.

'I've brought you a drink,' she said. 'You'll feel better. Try and drink this.'

There was no answer. Fred plunged her hands into the bucket. It was freezing, her fingers went numb.

She formed a cup and drew out some water.

'Here,' she said. 'Something to drink. Can you drink?'

She raised her cupped hands to the knight's mask and tipped it down the space where a mouth might be. The water disappeared greedily. She cupped her hands again, and gave him more and more, until the bucket was empty.

'Is that better?' she said.

The knight made no reply. Fred didn't mind. She felt a peculiar sort of patience, as though she were sure something would happen, if she could only wait long enough.

She looked at Rowley. His eyes were fixed on the knight with horror.

'What is it?' she said, clutching him.

'Fred! Look!' cried Rowley, rising from where he sat. 'The knight! He's disappearing!'

Fred looked. It was true. The knight wasn't running off, or slipping into a hole, but disappearing. What was once a great suit of rusting armour, at least twice the size of Rowley, was fading in front of them, like paint losing colour in the sun, or an illustration being erased from the page. The great blood-spattered gauntlets were no longer there, and now the arms were going, and now the legs, the boots, the chest with its rusted emblem . . .

'He's going away!' said Rowley hoarsely.

Fred and Rowley held tightly to each other's hand. It's like watching somebody die, thought Fred.

Now all that remained was the head – the visor, the mask, both noble and terrifying, strong and remote. And gradually, smudge by smudge, that too disappeared into nothing at all. Nothing remained.

The sky which had been dark with night turned to pink dawn, and with the dawn came the sound of high distant whistling, way up in heaven above their heads.

· 19 ·

The Golden Bridge

In the meantime, what had happened to Rabbit? Rabbit was sitting on the edge of the beach, his toes just touching the water. The gentle tide moved in and out. He was all by himself again – the children had run away in a hurry – nobody stopped to tell him where.

Rabbit thought they were very odd children. They were so playful and friendly – much more friendly than any children Rabbit had ever met before. Usually, Rabbit was nervous of other children – they teased him or wouldn't let him play or became angry with him or made him cry or laughed at him when he fell over. These children did none of those things – they were always smiling and holding out their hands towards him and asking him what he wanted to do.

Just now, they had all been flying kites on the

beach. It was wonderful! All the children had gathered together in their strange white robes, pointing up at the sky, hanging onto balls of string. Far away there were kites, hundreds of them, so far away you could no longer see the strings, just the coloured kites and their tails.

And then he had turned around to find that all the children had left without a sound, their kites with them. No one had said goodbye. They had just left him, in a moment, all alone on the beach.

So Rabbit had sat down on the sand and looked out at the endless beautiful water that stretched on and on, unlimited, unbounded. He was on the edge of nowhere.

I want to be somewhere, he thought, yearning. I do want to be somewhere.

He knew he didn't belong on the island. The children belonged there. But it wasn't for him. How could it be, when they came and went all the time? Rabbit couldn't live like that – he would rather be alone altogether, like Robinson Crusoe.

Rabbit stood up. He didn't have to stay on the island, after all. What had the little girl told him – there was a bridge? Well, a bridge, even a magic one, must lead to somewhere.

Now something remarkable happened. While Rabbit was thinking about the Golden Bridge and wondering where on earth it was and how he would reach it, he saw it, as though it had been there all the time, waiting for him to want it. It was a lovely curved sparkling span of a bridge, stretching from the edge of the beach across and over the waters, over to – where? There was such vapour in the air, Rabbit couldn't actually see where the bridge came to an end.

But it must, he thought trustingly. If it has a beginning, it will have an end.

He ran off towards the bridge, his little legs bouncing up and down on the sand. He felt light and powerful.

I am small, he thought, but I might win the Game.

It was a funny thing to come into his mind, because Rabbit did not normally ever think about winning. But now, suddenly, in his head the words were spinning: I can win! I can win!

At last he reached the bridge. The ends were sunk in the sand. Up close, the sheen had gone and settled into brown, and the curves had straightened. The bridge was as flat and long as a highway, made of wooden planks bound to each other with rope.

Rabbit turned and looked back at the island. He saw the trees, the rocks, the tall flowers.

I wish I could have said goodbye, thought Rabbit a little sadly, remembering the girl and her kindness.

A flock of birds came up suddenly from the deep

green branches in the middle of the island, flapping their bright wings, cawing.

'I'm sick of birds,' said Rabbit, turning away. And, braver than he had ever been, he stepped out onto the bridge.

The Ice Storm

'He's gone,' said Fred.

The whistling had stopped. She let go of Rowley's hand.

'It must have been the water that I gave him.'

She stood up and stepped into the place where the knight had been. 'I killed him!' she said, her voice cracking. 'I didn't mean to, Rowley, really I didn't.'

Rowley stood up, stunned and dizzy.

'I'm so sorry,' whispered Fred. 'I meant to help him.'

Rowley pressed his feet down in the empty space that had held the knight. His eyes, which had been so dull and distant, looked different, like somebody waking after a long sad sleep.

'I think you did help him, Fred,' he said at last.

There was a pause.

'I don't understand,' said Fred.

Neither did Rowley, really. 'I think,' he said, 'that you helped him. You helped him to leave.'

Rowley stopped. He could see that Fred still didn't understand.

'He was so lonely, Fred,' he said, trying to explain. 'All his friends had gone. He wanted me to lead him out. I didn't know how. But you did. When you gave him that water, you found the way for him.'

Fred felt tired. Rowley was making no sense to her. She shook her head.

'Shhhhhhh!' Rowley stood still in the forest, like an animal hunting.

'What?'

'The earth is trembling,' said Rowley. 'Can't you feel it?'

It was true, there was a slight shudder in the ground under their feet. The air was cold and damp.

'What is it?' said Fred.

Rowley could feel that he was becoming strong again, and brave.

'We can't stay,' he said. 'We've got to get out of here.'

'The peacocks,' Fred remembered. 'We'll follow them. They'll lead us somewhere safe.'

She looked around for the beautiful birds that had led her to Rowley, but they were nowhere to be seen.

Nor were the trees or the well. Lightning flashed. It was a storm, and there was no shelter. The sky began to break.

'Ouch!' shouted Rowley.

Something gave him a great blow on the back, and then another.

'It's ice!' screamed Fred.

And it was ice, great lumps of spiky ice as large as tennis balls, hurtling down from the sky, crashing to the ground, breaking into splinters.

'Come on!' Rowley grabbed Fred. He pulled her arms over to him. 'HOLD ONTO MY BACK!'

Rowley ran up and down on the spot. Were his little winged shoes still working? So dusty and dirty and miserable as they were. But they did – they lifted him into the air, Fred on behind him. The two children were carried up through the icy storm. Lightning cracked about them, and they were wet and battered with hail blows.

As they rose higher, the hail became thinner and turned to cold rain. Soon they were sailing past the rain as well, up to the ceiling of the world. The sun dried their clothes and their hair and they forgot about their bruises.

When Rowley looked down, he could see the Game laid out beneath him. He saw the twisting paths and the numbers, he saw the forests and the lakes and the islands. He saw the old city, he saw the maze, he saw the cold dungeon. He saw everything; everything was revealed to him.

This is what an eagle sees, he thought.

And it was remarkable, it was almost as though he had become an eagle, had always been an eagle, and he had forgotten what it was that a boy would see, and what it was to be a boy at all. He even forgot about Fred, hanging on his back. A strange and delightful sensation of safety engulfed him, like a baby in a mother's arms. He stretched out his arms and let himself fly.

Fred, on the other hand, was getting rather tired of hanging onto Rowley's waist. Her arms were aching and her head was itching but she didn't dare let go to scratch herself. She would have shouted out to Rowley, but there was no point as the noise of the rushing air was deafening.

She looked back down at the Game. It reminded her of how she had sat alone in the cubby, desperate to get in, and had seen a tiny Rowley and an even tinier Rabbit on the board. She could see the Game now quite clearly, even the edges of it, the borders where it came to an end. What lay beyond? she wondered. Is it floating, like us? Or perhaps it's resting on something, on a giant table, and there could be giant people staring down at it right now. Could giant eyes be

seeing me as I had seen Rabbit and Rowley?

But then, if that were true where did it end? Perhaps there was another even larger Game resting on an even larger table, being watched by even huger giants. And if that were true, thought Fred, frowning, surely it must work the other way as well – that there was a smaller Game than the one in their cubby, resting on a smaller table with even smaller people watching. How small and how large could it become? Perhaps it went on for ever in each direction, for ever and ever.

Fred felt a jolt through her body. There was Rabbit!

She pulled on Rowley, she pinched him, she tried to get his attention.

'Rowley – down there! It's Rabbit!'

But while their flight was calm, the air roared about them. Rowley didn't hear her.

'ROWLEY!' shouted Fred.

Poor little Rabbit! He was walking manfully across a long rickety bridge, his funny little legs marching up and down.

But what he seemed unaware of was that the bridge itself was collapsing at one end – the end towards which he was heading. There was a mountainside that was crumbling, and with it the moorings of the bridge. Rabbit was too far along to turn back, yet any moment now the bridge would fall and with it Rabbit into the sea below, which was far and deep and filled with icy thorns. They had to do something!

'It's Rabbit! We have to go down! He's in trouble!'

They could fly down, thought Fred, and she could grab his hand and they would fly up into the air and away. If Rowley could carry her, he could surely carry Rabbit.

'ROWLEY!'

She pummelled on his back with both her fists – and that was a mistake. Naturally enough, she let go of Rowley and began to spiral downwards.

As soon as Fred let go, Rowley felt the loss of her weight.

'Fred?' he said, swinging around.

Fred was hurtling down, like a plastic toy drawn to the drain of an emptying bath. Clouds were spinning about her in a whirlwind.

'Fred!' Rowley righted himself and then put his head and arms in a diving position to follow her down. He pedalled in the air with his feet and the wings of his shoes beat hard and he began to descend after her. But the closer he got, the further away she became.

And then Rowley saw Rabbit. He saw the collapsing bridge and the crumbling mountain. He pedalled faster, he gulped, he made swimming motions with his arms. If he could get there he could save them – if he could only get there in time!

But even as he pleaded with himself and every-thing around him, the worst happened. The bridge cracked and sighed and disappeared into the black ocean. Smoke rose up, black and thick as though the water were on fire.

· 21 ·

The Gates of Heaven

The roar of the skies softened. Rowley touched the ground. He stood on the banks of the lake where moments before he had seen the bridge collapse. The waters had closed over it, and were now swaying a little in a warm breeze. The mild blue waves shone. There was no dark fire, no smoke.

'I –' he began.

He stared down at his feet – there were the shoes, the wings quietly folded like a resting pigeon.

Had he seen what he had seen? Where was Fred? Where was Rabbit? Had they – and the thought struck him – have I won the Game?

He looked behind him, away from the water. Out stretched a field of bright green grass scattered with wildflowers. He could see the winding paths of the Game, he could see mountains and rivers, he could even see the walls of the old city in the distance.

And then he heard a sound, a tiny distant tinkling, like a fairy bell.

What's that? he wondered, and he rubbed his ears.

'Hallo?' he said, rather nervously. 'Is anyone there?'

The tinkling continued. There was something familiar about it, and sad as well, almost like somebody crying.

'Rabbit?'

Could it be Rabbit? Rowley's heart leapt. He ran towards the sound, up the flowered banks of the lake.

'Rabbit?' called Rowley.

It was someone crying! But where? There was nowhere to hide in the open fields.

He swung around on the spot until he was dizzy. He stumbled, pulled himself up, and then he saw him.

It was Rabbit, kneeling down, next to a pale rock.

'Oh, Rabbit!' said Rowley in relief, and tumbled over, putting an arm around his little shoulders.

Rabbit looked up. He gazed woefully at Rowley and said, 'Where've you been? I've been here for hours!'

'It's all right now, Rabbit,' said Rowley, giving him a squeeze. 'We're together now. It'll be all right.'

'How can it be all right?' wept Rabbit. 'Look at Fred!'

'Fred?'

Rowley stared. The pale rock was not a rock, it was

Fred. Fred lying flat on her back on the ground next to Rabbit. Her eyes were closed.

Rabbit sniffed, and wiped his face with his hand. He looked up at Rowley, frightened.

'I pulled her out,' he said. 'Out of the water – it was so cold, Rowley!'

'You pulled her out! How did you do that? She's twice as big as you.'

Rabbit's eyes were huge. 'I don't know,' he said. 'But I did and I brought her up here to dry. She's dry now, isn't she?'

Fred looked perfectly dry. She looked, in fact, as if she had had a wonderful bath because her hair and skin were shining and so clean. Rowley couldn't remember ever seeing Fred so clean. She looked – well, she looked very nice, Rowley thought in some surprise.

'But she won't wake up,' whispered Rabbit. 'It's been hours. I've tried to wake her but she won't get up.'

For a moment, the world became still. Rowley felt the breath stop in his throat. If I don't breathe soon, he thought, I will choke. But if I do –

He gulped. He knelt down and leant over Fred. He reached out a hand and touched her skin. He bent right down and put his cheek next to hers. He shut his eyes.

Then he sat up. He looked straight at Rabbit. 'She's dead,' he said.

'No,' said Rabbit.

There was a little silence in the warm wind.

Rowley said, in a voice like ash, 'She must have drowned.'

'No!' repeated Rabbit. 'I pulled her out. I saved her.'

'You tried to save her, Rabbit.' Rowley held Rabbit's hand, but he shook it off. 'You were too small. She –'

'She's not dead!' shouted Rabbit, jumping.

Rowley hid his face in his fingers. 'She's dead, Rabbit,' he said.

Rabbit punched him. He punched him with his little fists and he shouted, 'She can't be! She can't be dead! I can't bear it if she's dead.'

Rowley lifted his head. 'We just have to bear it,' he said. 'There's nothing else for us to do.'

Fred lay on the ground between them. Of course she was dead – how could he not have seen it at once? Her face – it was Fred's face, but it had no Fred in it. It was like a waxwork he had seen once of Sleeping Beauty; perfect and lovely with nothing there. Nothing that made Fred Fred. Even the waxwork, he remembered, had some mechanism that made Sleeping Beauty's chest rise and fall as though she were only sleeping, to show she was alive. But Fred was not breathing. She was not alive. She had fallen and drowned in that horrible sea. He had stretched out his arms to fly like a bird, and she had let go. He looked for a moment at his shoes. His magic winged shoes. He kicked them off and left his feet bare, like Rabbit.

Rowley's mind was very dark. He lay down on the ground, gazing at Fred. There were white flowers growing about her, and he reached out and slowly began to pick them, one by one. He broke off another and another. He laid them over Fred, like a blanket.

Rabbit watched him without moving. His little mild face was so angry, so tragic, Rowley couldn't look at him.

Rowley pulled off flower after flower, laying them over Fred, until at last only her poor dead face remained, surrounded by white as though snow had fallen over her.

'No!'

Rabbit's voice was so . . . so grown-up, it hardly seemed to be Rabbit.

'She's not dead!' said Rabbit. 'I told you – I can't bear it.'

Rowley was at a loss. He grasped for something to say. 'We have to,' he said helplessly. 'We just have to.'

'No!' Rabbit stamped his feet. 'I can't. That's it.'

'But –'

Rabbit was thinking hard. His forehead was creased. 'When – when you die,' he said, 'what happens to you?'

Rowley shook his head. 'Nothing happens to you,' he said. 'You're dead.'

'I know you're dead,' said Rabbit. 'But you go somewhere, don't you?'

'Well . . .' Rowley was older than Rabbit and didn't believe in as many things as he used to.

'You go to heaven!' said Rabbit. 'Don't you?'

Rowley said nothing. His head and his heart were aching.

'So we'll just have to go to heaven and get Fred back!' said Rabbit and he folded his arms as if to say – so, there!

'Oh, Rabbit.'

Rowley was so weary of everything. How he wished they had never got into the Game! He wished they had never seen it in the shop, never been to the shop, never formed the club, never been in the cubby, that the fence factory hadn't burnt down, that the parents had never wanted to fix the fences in the first place . . .

'Won't we?' persisted Rabbit.

'Rabbit,' Rowley tried. 'Look, Rabbit – even if there is heaven, there wouldn't be a heaven in a Game. This is a Game, remember? It's just a Game. There's no heaven here!'

'If it's just a Game,' replied Rabbit, 'why is Fred dead?'

The leaves rustled, there was a thudding sound as ripened fruit fell to the ground, like a horse softly galloping towards them. And then the eerie whistling from above, and wind.

The light was bright suddenly. Rowley blinked. Slowly, the light died down and shapes began to form.

'Oh!' cried Rabbit. 'Look!'

In front of them stood a gate. It was taller than the tallest building they had ever seen, and shinier than the brightest golden bowl. It must have been made of pure gold, and shaped into beautiful grand and stately arcs and linking squares and it stretched upwards and sideways into clouds.

'It's heaven!' whispered Rabbit. 'It's the gates of heaven.'

Even Rowley, who had thought he did not believe in heaven, knew that it must be. What else could these wonderful gates lead to?

'We can go in!' said Rabbit. 'You see, we can go and get Fred!'

Rowley trembled. He was so afraid – of what Rabbit wanted.

'Oh, Rabbit,' he muttered.

'We can, Rowley. Don't you see?'

Rabbit held up the string around his neck. 'My key! This is what my key is for – to open the gate! It must be!'

In Rabbit's fingers shone the tiny key. Rowley shook his head. How could Rabbit think that such a small thing would open something so grand and huge . . .

But Rabbit paid no attention to him. The little boy walked forward boldly to the high shiny gates, which were held together in the middle by what was clearly a lock.

Rabbit stopped in front of the gates and the world around them was filled with the most tremendous hush, as though every creature alive, that had ever lived, or indeed had never lived, were watching Rabbit, waiting to see what he would do.

Rabbit took the string from around his neck. The keyhole, which had seemed so far above his head, was now almost in reach. He stood up on his toes, stretching his arm, grasping the key tightly between his thumb and forefinger.

He reached, he stretched, he yearned, he wished, he wanted, he hoped, he had to put the key in the lock –

'There!'

It was in! And he turned it, not slowly, but with the quickest movement that Rowley scarcely saw it happen. And once the key was turned, the lock opened, and the gates swung apart.

· 22 ·

The End of the Game

So Rabbit and Rowley stepped inside the gates of heaven. They walked right into heaven itself.

What is heaven like? Nobody knows, and afterwards Rabbit and Rowley could not remember. They could only remember they had been there.

They didn't feel frightened. They had a funny sort of feeling that they had never felt before.

Maybe we feel dead, thought Rabbit. Maybe this is what it's like when you're dead.

The ground under their bare feet was soft and powdery, like snow, but it wasn't cold. Whiteness stretched out, flat and broad, on and on. There were no hills, no trees. Nothing.

We're not dead, Rabbit reminded himself. But if this is heaven and I know it is, where are all the dead people?

He walked on in front of Rowley. It was as though Rabbit had become the big one and Rowley the small one.

'Where is Fred?' wondered Rabbit out loud. 'And where is God?'

God should be there. God should be standing right there, waving kindly and saying welcome, tossing his long beard aside.

There was no one to answer these questions. Or was there? All around them was emptiness, but Rabbit had the strangest sensation of being surrounded by – by things. Things in the air.

They must be spirits, he thought. They must be invisible. But how would he find Fred to bring her back if she were invisible? He could call her name, he supposed, but there must be millions of Freds in heaven. What if they all wanted to come back with him? He could only take his own Fred.

Then he did feel frightened. What would he do with all that death, when he was so alive? They might be angry with him, those spirits, they might be jealous. They might remember what it was like to be alive and want to – he didn't know what they might want to do.

'There's no one here,' said Rowley.

Rabbit stood in the middle of the glistening empty space, his hands on his hips. 'Oh no,' he said. 'You're wrong. There're millions of people here. Millions and Millions.'

The air swayed and creaked.

Rowley said, 'Rabbit – look! There's something over there! On the ground!'

Rabbit looked. There was something in the powdery white, something small.

The two boys grabbed instinctively each other's hand. They moved forward towards it.

'It's an animal,' said Rowley. They came closer. 'It's been hurt.'

They reached the little creature lying quivering on the ground.

'It's a bird,' whispered Rabbit.

It was a small pale bird, lying on its side. Its wings shook as though in pain. Its eyes were closed.

'There's something around its neck,' said Rabbit, kneeling down.

Very gently, he reached out his fingers to the bird's neck. A piece of rough string was tied around it, and attached to that a scrap of paper. Rabbit bent down as low as he could, screwing up his eyes.

'It's a message,' he said. 'I can't read. Can you read it, Rowley?'

Rowley sat down next to him. The ground felt like nothing. We're in a big nothing, he thought.

He looked down at the paper around the neck

of the poor dying bird.

'I don't know what it says,' he said, puzzled. 'It's not letters that I know.'

Rabbit said, 'You can't read it?'

Rowley shook his head. 'I think it's a different language.'

Rabbit thought for a moment.

'It must be the language of heaven,' he said at last. 'They must speak a different language here.'

Rowley was gazing at the bird. He wondered what had happened to it. Gingerly, he put out his forefinger and stroked the down of its breast. Its tiny heart was beating fiercely.

'Perhaps we should nurse it,' he said, hesitating. 'It's so alone, poor thing.'

'Could you pick it up?' asked Rabbit, his eyes widening. 'It might peck you.'

'It might.'

Rowley bent right down over the little winged creature. Its eyes opened. They were round and dark and deep. They were imploring and trusting. Rowley very gently put his hands about the folded wings and lifted it up. The bird fluttered its wings slightly, then stopped and rested its head against Rowley's arm.

'Oh, it's beautiful,' whispered Rabbit, stroking it.

Now there were three of them. Rowley and Rabbit and the poor little bird. The sky looked like sunset, but there was no sun, and there was no end of the earth for the sun to sink into.

'You know,' said Rowley after a while, pointing to the paper around the bird's neck. 'Perhaps it's not a message. Perhaps those letters are its name.'

He put his head down, right next to the bird's face. 'Maybe if I just try to read it,' he said.

And very softly, as best he could, he spoke the word written on the paper.

'But –' said Rabbit, 'I know that word!'

He did know the word, he was sure he had heard it before!

'Do you?' said Rowley. 'What is it? Is it a name?'

Rabbit didn't know. He couldn't remember – just darkness in the cubby and a whisper in his ear, a word.

It was a magic word, it must have been. On hearing it, the bird was visited by an extraordinary surge of strength. It rose up from where it had been lying, beating its wings noisily, powerfully. It flew above their heads. They leapt to their feet, astonished.

The bird twirled around and swooped. It opened its mouth and cawed. It was as though it had been born again. It grew in size, its wings were huge!

'It's the Goose!' breathed Rabbit.

It was the Goose! Almost golden, so grand! Rabbit and Rowley stood watching it circling above their heads, swooping up and down, all the time whistling and beating its great and wonderful wings.

'The Goose will help us,' said Rabbit. 'It will help us find Fred and make her alive.'

Did the Goose hear? It made no sign, but both boys felt that it had. Up and down and around it flew, sometimes so close that they felt the brush of its passing wing.

'Fred!' shouted Rabbit. 'Where is Fred? We want Fred!'

Both the boys put their hands up to their mouths to make their voices louder against the high weird whistling of the Goose.

'Please let us have Fred!' they called upwards. 'Please let us have her back! Please!'

Millions of things rushed by them and around them. Was one of them Fred? They couldn't see anything. Rowley reached out his hands, trying to grasp hold.

'Oh, please!' he cried. 'Please give us a second chance!'

The Goose became still, hovering above them, as though it were thinking, deciding something. The whistling stopped.

'Please,' said Rowley, his voice dropping. 'Please.'

And then, without looking in their direction, the Goose flew in a flash right up into the sky and all that remained was the airy sound of the flapping of wings.

· *23* ·

Home

There were three children: Fred, Rowley and Rabbit. Fred was sitting on the floor in the Salvation Army shop next to Rabbit, pulling on the grey elephant moneybox. He was holding onto it equally tight. Rowley sat in the middle of them. On the carpet next to Rabbit, laid out two by two, were the little felt animals of the Noah's Ark. The Game of the Goose was in its box at Fred's feet.

Fred and Rabbit and Rowley stared at each other. They were like statues.

And then, as though they suddenly recognised each other, the expressions in their faces changed. Fred and Rabbit let go the plastic elephant and it clattered and rolled over on the ground.

'Oh!' said Fred, sounding dazed. She rubbed her forehead. Something had happened to her, too many things, but she didn't know what or how. She looked down at the floor and saw the Game.

'Oh,' she said again. She had wanted it very much. She could remember wanting it more than anything. But not more than anything, in the end.

She took a deep breath of wonderful air. She felt very weak and strong at the same time.

'Rabbit?' she said.

Rabbit looked up. Fred pointed at the Noah's Ark.

'Come on, Rabbit. Go and pay for it and let's go home.'

She stood up, slinging the shopping bag of milk, bread and bananas over her shoulder. She didn't look down at the Game again. She walked right away from it, towards the door.

Rowley began to pick up the little animals, putting them inside the cloth bag.

'Come on, Rabbit,' he said. 'Buy it. You can play with it at home.'

Rabbit's brain didn't feel quite right. He watched as Rowley packed up the Noah's Ark. Could he really have it? Could it be true? It looked like it was. He picked up his moneybox.

Rowley put the bag on the counter. Rabbit emptied the elephant next to it, and the coins formed a little pile.

'What's all this?' growled the man behind the

counter, looking up over his newspaper.

'It's my life savings,' said Rabbit.

'He wants to buy the Noah's Ark,' said Rowley.

'Aah.' The man nodded. He put down his newspaper. Rabbit held his breath. Would it be enough? The man picked up two of the coins and said to Rabbit, 'Put the rest back. Save it for another day.'

'Oh!'

Rabbit was so surprised he forgot to say thank you, but the man didn't seem to mind and went back to reading his newspaper. Rowley helped Rabbit scoop up the rest of the money and put it through the slit in the plastic elephant.

Fred was standing at the door, looking out. She couldn't stay inside the shop a moment longer. She felt so very odd, so full up. As though she had eaten an enormous banquet but couldn't recall a single dish.

'Hurry up, will you?' she shouted impatiently at the boys.

What were they doing in there? She smelt the summer clouds moving above her and making shadows on the street. She wanted to throw out her arms and run and then leap into deep water and sink and float like a starfish.

Finally Rabbit and Rowley emerged. Rabbit had two things to carry now: his moneybox and his Noah's Ark, so he couldn't hold anyone's hand.

'Well, just stick near me, all right?' said Fred, and she couldn't help smiling at him.

They stood together at the side of the road, waiting for the cars to stop. A warm breeze blew around the corner over them. Suddenly the air was filled with millions of tiny fluffy flying things, windborne seeds spinning about them.

The children raised their hands, trying to catch the things in their fingers but they blew here and there and away. There was a break in the traffic and they ran across the road, laughing and flapping their arms.

When they reached the other side, Rowley said, 'Look, Rabbit, there's something in your hair.'

Rabbit put his hand up to his head. His fingers closed around a long white and yellow feather, like a quill.

'What is it?' he said, wondering, showing them.

'It's a feather,' said Fred.

None of them spoke for a moment. They were all thinking about the very same thing. Their minds were bursting with what had happened to them, but nobody knew what to say.

'I think it means you won, Rabbit,' said Rowley at last. 'Don't you think, Fred?'

'I won?' said Rabbit, not believing his ears.

'I think it must,' said Rowley.

'I won the Game?' repeated Rabbit.

He looked at Fred. Fred would know.

Fred put out a finger to touch the feather. How it shone in the sunlight! 'I think he's right,' she said. 'It must mean that.'

'But how did I win?' asked Rabbit. 'What did I do?'

'I think you won,' said Fred slowly, 'because you had the most hope.'

The feather lay in Rabbit's small hand. They looked at it, all three of them. Then Rabbit closed his fingers around it and put it in his pocket.

That was the last time the children ever spoke about the Game, either between themselves or with anyone else. They walked home, each one of them back into their own house. A silence fell over them, like the silence of a deep and mysterious ocean.

When Rabbit got home, he went into his bedroom and put the feather under his pillow. Then he lay down on the bed and went straight to sleep.

Rowley went and sat on the back step of his house, and fed Jemima Puddleduck. He gave her a carrot and some lettuce leaves and he stroked her furry back. He felt very quiet.

Fred ran outside and jumped on her trampoline. She jumped so high and for so long that when at last her mother called her in for dinner, the whole earth felt springy beneath her feet, as though she were walking on a cloud.

All that summer holidays, the three children played together in their one huge backyard.

They hit balls and ran around and dressed up and played cards and read comics and ate apples. Sometimes they fought with each other, but mostly it was too hot and big to fight much and they lay around on the grass until they forgot what had made them angry.

By the end of the holidays, the fences went up again. The factory reopened, the parents got back on the phone, and people came in trucks and dug and hammered and what had been one huge backyard became three small ones again.

But the children found cracks and holes and loose boards, because children do, and they ran in and out of each other's gardens almost as though the fences weren't there. And Rowley's father cut a hole in the roof of the cubby and put glass over it, so that there was a wide window and the light streamed down from the ceiling and they didn't need a candle any more. And Jemima Puddleduck made herself a nest there and grew very fat and happy.

Fred, Rowley and Rabbit never talked about the Game, not even when they grew up. But none of them forgot it. What had happened to each of them had happened to all of them and they knew it for ever.

About the author

URSULA DUBOSARSKY was born in Sydney, Australia, the third child in a family of writers. She spent much of her childhood knocking on walls with the hope of discovering secret passages that she had read about in British adventure stories. Today, Ursula is widely regarded as one of the most talented and original writers in Australia. She has won many awards, including, most recently, the 2006 Victorian Premier's Literary Award and NSW Premier's Literary Award for *Theodora's Gift,* and the 2006 Queensland Premier's Literary Award for *The Red Shoe*, which was also shortlisted for the 2007 CBC Book of the Year: Older Readers.

Ursula lives in Sydney with her husband Avi, her daughter Maisie, and sons Dover and Bruno. She has recently completed her PhD in English literature at Macquarie University.